A Shadows Journey

Prides Desire

DEVIN MANBECK

Vanity and pride are different things, though the words are often used synonymously. A person may be proud without being vain. Pride relates more to our opinion of ourselves, vanity to what we would have others think of us.

-Jane Austen

Contents

Prelude to the Journey

Hidden in the depths of hell in a random cave lies a door. That door leads to the home of the original sinner and the lost great warrior of hell, Eve. She is currently in the room in her home that she uses for training and exercise. The room contains perfectly cut soul rocks for the floor and dulled obsidian covering the walls of the whole room. Each wall has what looks to be an apple carved into them by some kind of blade, most likely a sword. This room that usually has a scent of obsidian is currently filled with the scent of sweat and metal. The reason for that is because in this room she is finishing her pupil's training in her sword and martial arts fighting style. When their swords clash against each other a great force can be felt through the room. Her pupil will be fighting a strong group of devils and must be ready for the task at hand. Her pupil has only been training with her for one and a half weeks, but due to his task being of great importance she put him through her accelerated crash course. She believed her pupil was the type that mostly kept to himself, but learned quickly that wasn't entirely true.

The pupil goes by Shadow, with his true name to remain unknown even to his master. The pupil's name isn't the only thing shrouded in mystery. For personal reasons the pupil keeps his face and hair covered so few people other than himself have seen his true face. Even Eve has only seen his actual face only once. She noticed that he has a great talent for picking up training and techniques very quickly. She could tell that he was almost a perfect pupil to train. The only setback is that he was hindered by personal problems before becoming her pupil. He took to the accelerated training from his master with great strides toward his goal. His training with his master has made great progress even if it's been over a short amount of time. The accelerated crash course Eve's using on him should have lasted twice as long as it has. The reason for that is that he always keeps his eyes on who he's facing to know what they will do and reacts to it almost like he can read their mind or aura. He also pushed himself even harder, especially for the accelerated crash course. Even with such amazing talent his greatest weakness is himself. He now faces his master in a battle as a test to gauge his strength and skill to see if he's ready. This is a test that he is determined to pass no matter what.

"You've really improved with your technique, Shadow," says Eve proudly.

"Thank you Master, it's all thanks to your teachings," says Shadow. *I know I couldn't manage this much on my own,* thinks Shadow.

Their swords collide one more time with enough strength that the force pushes them back.

Eve puts away her tantalum training sword. "We're done Shadow, you've passed the final test," says Eve.

Shadow is still breathing a little bit hard from the last strike, but he still keeps his sword out and stays on guard. *Are we finally done with training? No, Master looks like she's ready to go for another strike*, thinks Shadow.

"You won't fool me with that trick again Master!" says Shadow with slight anger in his voice.

Eve lunges at him. "Good, you caught on to my trick easily and prepared yourself for my attack this time. You seem to be getting used to them now," says Eve as she draws her training sword to strike again. *Knowing when his enemies are lying will help him stay alive down here*, thinks Eve.

With a quick slash Shadow knocks Eve's sword out of her hand mid-unsheathing. As her sword lands on the ground Shadow places one of the bladed sides of his sword near his master's neck. "Did I pass now, Master?" asks Shadow in an exasperated tone.

"Yeah, it looks like you are good enough to go out there and not get killed by just anyone," said Eve calmly with the sword still next to her neck.

Shadow lowers his sword and gives a sigh of relief that his training is over.

As Eve picks up her training sword she points to the door out of the room with her free hand. "Let's go over to the garden. I have a gift to give you for completing your training," says Eve.

A gift, thinks Shadow with excitement and worry. As Eve walks to the door Shadow sheaths his sword and follows after his master.

They leave the training room and enter a room that looks like the outside but is still inside. The floor has artificial grass that could easily pass for the real thing. The upper walls and ceiling are painted blue to resemble the day sky with lights that can change the amount of light to what time of day Eve wants. Lining the top of the wall are symbols going around the whole room. There are two fake trees made of stone that she uses for storage along the walls on different ends of the room. Going around the walls of the room to connect the two trees is a snakelike decoration slithering around the room. The whole place smells like a vast floral garden giving a calming atmosphere. A perfect place to relax after coming right out of training.

As they enter the room Eve stops and lets out a little awkward laugh. "Hmm, even though you have currently finished your training I doubt you would still last very long if I took you more seriously and used Mada instead of this training sword," says Eve, pointing to one of the trees that holds her sword. The sword is her personal broadsword with a red metal blade and a green metal-and-wood handle.

Shadow looks at her sword and then looks back at his master. "Well you also said that it wouldn't be fair to train me with that right away," responds Shadow. *She probably knew that I wasn't worth taking seriously for my training,* thinks Shadow in a slightly depressed tone.

"I'm aware of what I said, I'm just making a point. Maybe when you get some real battle experience we can take your training to the next level," says Eve. *Which shouldn't take long since he's already made so much progress in only roughly eleven days,* thinks Eve with pride for her pupil. "Though that can wait for later. For now it's time you get your gift for passing my test and for you to start what you came down to hell for," says Eve as she points to Shadow. "Though before we do that let's change out of our training clothes first," says Eve.

"Understood. I will also gather my belongings so I can get ready to leave," responds Shadow. *I should be ready to leave so I don't impose on my master anymore than I already have,* thinks Shadow in a worrisome tone.

"That won't be necessary right now, you should wait till tomorrow. I can see it's almost nightfall thanks to Medea, and nights in hell are far darker than on earth. You won't be able to see where you're going. You will stay here till daybreak before taking off," says Eve.

Shadow looks over to look at Medea. Atop one of the fake trees is Eve's spirit beast Medea, sleeping. The creature resembles an owl with heron wings. It always seems to know what time it is despite not going outside. Eve is able to use her to help tell the time. Shadow nods to what Eve said and the two of them head off to get changed.

The two return to their rooms to get changed. Shadow enters the room that he's staying in while training. The room is somewhat bare with only a bed, a bookshelf with some books on it, a couple of wooden crates used for storage, and Shadow's duffle bag with all of his stuff that he brought with him. After grabbing a change of clothes Shadow returns to the garden where his master is waiting. Eve is dressed in a sundress that makes it look and feel like it's made of leaves. With Shadow, everything that he wears is black: shoes, jeans, shirt, and gloves. He also wears a full black head mask that covers his whole head and reaches down to his neck.

Eve looks at Shadow and what he's wearing. "Have you ever thought of dressing in any other colors, Shadow?" asks Eve. *Mainly that mask makes me feel like it's going to cause misunderstandings with the devils here, especially in this territory*, thinks Eve.

Shadow looks at himself. "Sorry, I just feel more comfortable in this color," says Shadow. *I guess the way I dress is odd if Master even thinks so,* thinks Shadow in a depressed tone.

Eve notices Shadow looking sad from her comment, *Crap, it looks like I accidentally upset him again. I really need to watch what I say to him. He already has low self-esteem as is*, thinks Eve in a worried tone. Noticing this, she quickly changes the subject. "Well it's fine, I'm not one to question someone's taste in clothes. Anyways, here is the gift that I promised you," says Eve, handing Shadow a thin box.

I rarely get gifts so I really appreciate that Master is giving me this even though she doesn't have to, thinks Shadow. Shadow takes the box and proceeds to open it. He sees a light brown cloak with black lines erratically placed all over it. "Thank you Master," says Shadow with a slightly confused gesture. *It looks nice, but what is the design supposed to be? Is it a design that I'm just too dense to understand?* thinks Shadow.

"It's meant to resemble bark from a tree," explains Eve.

Shadow looks back at the cloak. "OOHHH now I understand. I'm sorry for not catching that sooner Master," responds Shadow. "How did I not notice that earlier? I'm really stupid," whispers Shadow with great self-doubt.

Eve takes a closer look at her present to Shadow and realizes something: it's the wrong gift. "Whoops, I gave you the wrong cloak. That's the one I made that I messed up the design on," says Eve.

Did Master really make this cloak for me? thinks Shadow.

Eve starts to reach for the box that the cloak is in. "I have a better one I made that looks much nicer," says Eve.

Shadow holds his hand up to tell her to stop. "No, this cloak's fine, Master. I appreciate this gift. I even like it more knowing it was a failed one," says Shadow.

Eve is a little shocked by what he said, but is glad that he likes her gift. *Oh, maybe he thinks the imperfections make it more unique,* thinks Eve.

A screwed-up cloak for a screwup like me, thinks Shadow.

Shadow puts his new cloak on. "It feels great, thank you Master," says Shadow.

Eve looks at her pupil with a smile. "I'm glad that you like it, but your gift isn't finished yet," says Eve.

Shadow looks at her with confusion. "What do you mean it's not finished? It looks fine to me," questions Shadow.

Eve walks behind Shadow and places her hand on his back. Shadow becomes very tense from his master both being behind him and having her hand on his back. "Sorry Shadow, I know you don't like being in this situation, but I need to do this while you are wearing the cloak. It should only take a few seconds to finish up your gift. So just try to deal with it until I'm done please," says Eve.

Shadow nods and stands as still as he can while still tensed up. Shadow then sees a light coming from behind him which puts him more on edge. *Oh god what in hell is Master doing behind me?!* thinks Shadow in a very worried manner.

Eve takes her hand off Shadow's back. "Aaand I'm finished, now your gift is complete," says Eve. Eve notices that Shadow is still very tense from what she did. "Sorry again about that Shadow. I know you don't like people being behind you or touching your back, but it was the only way I could add the final touches to your gift," says Eve.

Shadow relaxes. "It's fine Master. What did you do to the cloak?" asks Shadow.

"I added two things to it. First a seal that will act as a space to hold anything you pick up to make your journey easier without you being weighed down. The other is a defense spell to keep someone from trying to steal this cloak from you. That's why I needed to do it while you wore it, so it could be connected to only you," explains Eve.

Shadow looks at Eve. "Is the latter spell really that necessary, Master?" asks Shadow.

"Trust me, beings down here will try to steal basically anything if they have the chance. It happens more often than you think," explains Eve.

"Ok Master, I'll be sure to be on high alert for that on my journey," says Shadow with a slight look of worry. *I already have experience with people like that already from before even coming here,* thinks Shadow.

"I'd also give you one of my swords too, but I'm sure you could tell that they're all in rough shape after all the sparring that we did. In the condition they're in right now they would probably break on the first demon, monster, and/or devil that tried to pick a fight with you," says Eve.

"It's alright, I'll try to be careful. Besides, I learned enough from your hand-to-hand training that I should be able to make it to the nearest town or city to get a new sword," answers Shadow. *Hopefully anyways,* thinks Shadow.

"Ok, now that that is settled, let's get dinner ready. I'll be sure you have something nice before you head out at daybreak," says Eve. Eve then starts heading to a door that leads to her home's kitchen, with Shadow following behind her.

The kitchen has wooden floors which give it a different feel compared to the grassy area of the garden. The walls are covered in vines that can produce a variety of plant-based foods which Eve uses for cooking and even uses to hold her cooking utensils. Like the garden lining the top of the wall, there are symbols going around the whole room. In the middle of the room is a table that looks like it can fit four to six people, which Shadow originally found strange and unusually large for his master to use, but he didn't question it. There's an icebox next to the far wall. It's maintained with a magic stone and comes up just past Shadow's waist to keep some food preserved. On top of it is a cabinet that holds dishes, silverware, and nonperishable foods. Next to both is a stove/oven also maintained with magic stones, which Eve is heading toward. Lastly there are three ways out of the room. Two doors, one to the garden and one to the cave that exits the house, and a staircase to personal rooms.

After both of them enter the kitchen Eve starts preparing the main dish while Shadow prepares a salad and the table.

"So have you gotten used to them by now, Shadow?" asks Eve.

"Yes I have, Master Eve, more or less. They feel completely natural to me at this point," answers Shadow while rubbing one of his eyes over his mask.

"That's good, I wasn't sure if they were still irritating for you or not. It's been a really long time since I had to perform that procedure," says Eve.

Eventually they finish the preparations and get to sit down to have their last meal together for the time being. Their meal is a fig salad and whole wheat noodles with meat chunks with a mushroom sauce, with pomegranate juice for Shadow and wine for Eve.

"Since it's your last meal here I thought I'd make your favorite dish that you had here," says Eve.

"How did you know this was my favorite dish, Master?" asks Shadow.

"Simple, with any other dish you always tried to finish it as fast as possible, but with this dish you're actually taking your time to enjoy it," answers Eve.

"Oh sorry, it's just a force of habit," says Shadow in a sad tone as he rolls up his mask. He rolls up his mask just high enough for him to eat. Shadow's now exposed neck reveals it's covered with a large faded bruise.

Eve looks at Shadow's neck with an uncomfortable look, unsure if it was self-inflicted or not while rubbing her neck. "I'm kind of glad you came down the way you did. Otherwise you might have chosen to come here the official way. Though that doesn't mean what you did wasn't reckless. I mean who just jumps through a portal that a devil came out from. You're lucky your eyes were the only part of you that needed replacing," says Eve.

Shadow sheepishly nods, feeling uncomfortable knowing Eve makes a valid point and is thinking about the bruise around his neck. "I understand Master, but my options were limited at that time. My friend was abducted and I had to follow them otherwise I might've never seen them again," says Shadow.

Now Eve starts feeling more uncomfortable from talking about it. *I better change the subject to something else. He's already under a lot of stress. I don't want to add more to it than I already have,* thinks Eve. "So anyways, do you have everything ready for tomorrow? I don't want you to head out and then worry that you forgot something," asks Eve.

Shadow nods to her question. "Yes, I never really unpacked and only took out what I needed at the time. I didn't want to make a mess in your home. You've already done so much for me. More than most people I know have. I only wish that I could've done more to repay you," says Shadow.

Eve becomes irritated by what Shadow says and reaches over the table to lightly smack the top of his head. "Now stop that, I already told you that you shouldn't be so down on yourself and trying to take everything onto yourself. Geez, I thought I got through to you when you tried to do all the chores yourself when you first got here. On top of your harsh and rushed training. Though I guess eleven days can't take out the years of conditioning that you've been through so easily," says Eve.

Shadow droops his head in sadness. "I'm sorry for disappointing you Master," apologizes Shadow. *Once again I disappointed Master Eve. I should've known that I wasn't good enough to be her student,* thinks Shadow.

Eve is getting more irritated at Shadow. "Hey I told you to stop that already. You haven't disappointed me one bit Shadow. So stop with all of your self-doubt, at least around me," says Eve.

Shadow only nods at Eve, not wanting to look her in the eye. "I'll try Master," says Shadow.

The two of them finish their meal and get ready for bed.

Nighttime Stories

A few hours have passed since Shadow and Eve went to their rooms to get some sleep. This is one of the few times that Shadow willingly removes his mask completely as it's so dark his face is still hidden from sight. Shadow just lays in his bed looking at the ceiling. He has been continually going in and out of sleep since he got into bed. The longest bit of sleep he got since getting to bed lasted around twenty to thirty minutes. It was not solely from the worry about his friend or about departing at daybreak. For Shadow this was a regular routine for him. Over the years Shadow's mind and body started this strange sleep cycle as a sort of defense. When he's sleeping somewhere he feels is dangerous or unknown to him he will have bursts of sleep with most lasting around a minute. The longer he can stay asleep in a location the more he's grown comfortable and secure in the location. Though that doesn't mean that his sleep isn't affected by his anxiety about everything.

Feeling uneasy, Shadow decides to get out of bed. He thinks that he might try to get some last minute training in before he has to depart. Shadow puts his mask back on, though knowing he doesn't need to, and heads down the stairs into the kitchen which is all pitch-black. Shadow is able to navigate himself through the darkness with ease. He's used to walking around with little to no visibility. Over the years Shadow has also developed a sort of night vision. After making it down the stairs to the kitchen with ease Shadow notices some light coming from the bottom of the door leading to the garden. *Huh, were the lights left on? No, the light coming from the door doesn't look like a lot. Maybe it's a candle. Is Master inside there? Maybe she couldn't sleep or something. I should be careful going in if she doesn't want to be bothered or if she's asleep*, thinks Shadow, slowly approaching the door.

Shadow slowly opens the door and sees Eve. She's sitting in a chair looking through a book. She has a nightstand right next to her with a candle shaped like a tree providing the light. Eve looks up and sees that the door is open and can tell Shadow is looking in on her. "You couldn't sleep either, Shadow? I guess I can't blame you. Do you want to take a seat with me? We can keep each other company till we can go to sleep. Come in, I'll pull out a chair for you," says Eve as she stands up.

Eve sets the book down and walks to the storage tree. She pulls out a chair similar to the one she was sitting on. After setting it across from her seat she gestures for Shadow to sit down. Though hesitant at first, Shadow takes a seat. After sitting the two stare at each other in silence. Feeling awkward about the situation, Shadow and Eve try to think of something to talk about. The two look at the candle that has been giving them the only bit of light and choose that. "That candle looks really nice, did you make that, Master?" asks Shadow in a panicked tone.

"Yes, it's just one of the many hobbies and skills that I've picked up and developed over the many years. It helps pass the time and helps keep me from going mad with boredom," answers Eve.

After she answers, the two of them go back to the awkward silence. They both then remember the book that Eve was looking through. "So Master, what is that book you're reading? Is it an entertaining read? Though given the size it doesn't look like a normal novel. Is it actually a scrapbook or something?" rambles Shadow in a panicked tone.

Eve slightly giggles at how Shadow is awkwardly trying to start a conversation and panicking about it. "Yes actually, it is Shadow. I like to go through it when I finish training a student. It helps fill me with nostalgia and joy about my previous students. I even have images from my time during armageddon. Though those times are less enjoyable to remember most of the time," says Eve.

Shadow becomes surprised by what Eve said. "Wait you said Armageddon. Are you saying that it already happened and that you fought in it? How is that possible Master? It's supposed to be the final battle between good and evil. Does that mean that Judgment Day is coming or has it already happened?" asks Shadow while panicking.

Eve gets out of her chair and places a hand on top of Shadow's head to try and calm him down. "Calm down Shadow, it's not as bad as you think. Armageddon was just the name that was used for the war between hell and heaven. It's not some final battle. It was just a war, though probably larger than most wars that people on earth have seen in ancient and modern history. So I guess I can see why humans can misinterpret the situation. Though here in hell it's just seen as an old war that is taught as part of our history. Since we need something to talk about since you're too riled up to get any sleep, how about I give you a summary of the war and my involvement in it?" says Eve.

Shadow nods as he tries to calm down. Eve sits back down to get comfortable to tell Shadow her story. "Well to begin with, before the war there were several different realms of both of what is considered hell and heaven. For some reason the rulers of the hell realms started battles against one another. I'm not sure what the actual reason was and personally I don't care at this point. One of the most agreed upon reasons is they got greedy and wanted control of the other realms. At that point in the war they only had volunteers fighting their battle. They even tried bribing humans under their rule to also fight for them, with promises ranging from being brought back to life to getting a title and land," says Eve.

Shadow tilts his head in confusion about this. "Why were they bribing them? Couldn't they have forced them to fight for them?" asks Shadow.

Without missing a beat Eve looks at Shadow. "At the time there was an agreement between the rulers of the different underworld realms from before all this that any soldiers should be voluntary. I guess it was their way of proving they were better by showing how many soldiers actually want to fight for them. Though I didn't care and refused to help them no matter how good the compensation was. Though that didn't stop them from trying to get me to join multiple times. Anyways back to the history lesson. Eventually the heavenly realms caught wind of the underworld's civil war and chose to try and intervene. From what I've been told they wanted to stop them only because their fighting was starting to affect earth as well. I'm guessing they felt that they were the only ones who could stop it. Apparently, their plan was to stop the fighting immediately and have things go back to normal, but that's not what happened. All they did was make things a thousand times worse. All it did was make the battles grander in scale. Though they did stop them from fighting each other. That's because after the heavenly realms got involved all of the underworld realms aligned against them, turning what was in a way like a civil war between the different underworld realms to armageddon," says Eve.

Shadow continued to listen to Eve and started wondering about her while all of this was going on. "Master, I'm sorry to interrupt you again, but I was wondering, what were you doing while all of this fighting was going on? You said they tried to make you join multiple times. How were they able to get you to join them?" asks Shadow.

Eve slouched back more in her chair, looking through the room. "Basically the same as what I do now. I lived in a secluded area away from all the fighting. I was given that area from the shitty snake that damned me here in the first place. He basically did it out of pity for damning me for eternity because of a bet he had with that old bastard that kicked me out of paradise from eating a single fucking fruit from a certain tree," says Eve in an enraged tone.

"Huh, you getting kicked out of Eden was because of a bet? Did they actually tell you it was a bet Master?" asks Shadow.

"Yeah, I was told about it directly from the devil that gave me my original home. He even did it with a smug look on his face to look down on me. Since I'm just a soul now I'm basically immortal so I stayed there from when I was given it till after armageddon. While I was down here I filled my time with training and hobbies to pass the time to not go insane from boredom. I guess my talents were so impressive that they wanted to recruit me, but since I didn't owe them anything I refused. They didn't learn their lesson and during the whole time of the civil war and the beginning of armageddon they would visit me to try and recruit me. That kept happening, with me getting more and more irritated with them each time. By the time they asked me for the last time I gave them an earful using less-than-ladylike language. Sadly the next time I was visited about it I wasn't given a choice and was forced against my will to fight. They applied a special mask that was made for the war that essentially made me a slave to them and I couldn't go against what they ordered while it had a hold on me," answers Eve in a somber tone.

Shadow quickly notices that what he asked about was a touchy topic and feels bad. "I'm sorry Master, I didn't mean to have you talk about such a painful memory," says Shadow in a slight panicked tone.

Eve looks at Shadow and smiles, knowing that he didn't mean any harm by his question. "It's fine, I would have gotten there whether you asked about it or not. So then, let me continue the story. First let me just blow through a couple of things between where I left off and my enslavement. Basically with battles getting more intense the rulers of the underworld realms that were once fighting against each other decided that the best way to destroy their new enemy was to merge themselves all together and become a god with power never seen before. This unfortunately also came with the result of the different underworld realms merging together into the hell you see now. Personally I don't know the thought process that led to that, but it worked for them in the end. Of course, the rulers of the heavenly realms responded by doing the same thing and the same result happened. After that the battles got worse and they had to switch from voluntary soldiers to drafting soldiers whether they wanted to or not. That's around the time when the amalgamation of the rulers came to my house and forced me to fight for them. After that everything for a while was just a blur until I was freed. Though apparently I was a great asset for the war thanks to all my training. I won every battle I took part in nearly single-handedly. Though that didn't change the fact that I was still just a slave to them," says Eve.

"So how were you freed Master?" asks Shadow.

Eve gave a slight smirk from Shadow's question. "Well, that happened after I was reunited with Adam. You see, after I was sent to hell he was taken to heaven. I'm guessing those stupid gods thought that we weren't punished enough and decided to keep us apart after we died. Hard to say why exactly they did that to be honest. Personally I think it was one last 'fuck you two' after what happened in eden. Anyways he was also forced to fight for heaven's side against his will just like me. The type of weapon that he used during his battle was a lance or a rapier. He was used basically as a response to me and was just as powerful. Just like me he was also bound by a slave item. Though instead of a special mask his was a metal collar around his neck and metal shackles around his wrists. During one of the battles we were both forced to take part in, the two of us clashed with each other by sheer coincidence. The amount of force and power from our clash was able to send out a massive shock wave, knocking everyone else far away out of view. I'm not sure how exactly, but this caused our slave items to deactivate. Realizing I was free I took my mask off and saw Adam for the first time in who knows how long. Adam also recognized me and the two of us just stood there and teared up, overcome with feelings of happiness. Unfortunately reality had to come and ruin the moment. Adam's collar and shackles started to reactivate so thinking quickly I swung at them and destroyed them to free him completely. Soon after that I started to hear those blown away heading toward us. So Adam and I ran and hid to keep from being found. After the two of us were in a safe location we then set up a resistance to fight both hell and heaven. We started recruiting from both sides that were sick of how they were treated from their side. There were two recruits who were a major help to our side. First was a devil named Kaas that developed as a blacksmith just as good if not better than the gods. He made great weapons for us, even my own sword in the case right there. I'm sure you'll meet him eventually, Shadow. The other was an archangel named Simon that joined us out of respect for Adam and myself more than his own god. After everything, he was made into a messenger between the leaders of hell and heaven. You might see him while you take on the sins, but that's more up to luck," says Eve.

Shadow nods, happily thinking of those two. "Wow you must really trust them to say such a thing about those two Master," says Shadow.

"Personally I only really trust Kaas. That angle on the other hand was tolerated more than anything. He seemed more like a brownnoser than an ally and got on my nerves constantly just by the way he talked," says Eve, slightly annoyed.

"How did the way that he talked get on your nerves Master?" asks Shadow.

"Well even though he sucked up to me and Adam, it always seemed like he was up to something. It almost felt like he was going to stab us in the back for his own gain when given the chance. He even started wearing this odd choker that he said he supposedly took from a fallen enemy. Which I found both disgraceful and tacky, especially since the thing would sometimes light up slightly. Because of stuff like that I never let my guard down around him; he was still a valuable ally though. He taught me things that I couldn't have learned in my isolation. He even taught me the procedure that I used for your eyes," answers Eve.

Shadow places his left hand near his eyes. Shadow looks back to his master. "So what happened to them, Master?" asks Shadow.

"Well I can get to that after finishing the story since I'm nearly done anyways," says Eve.

Shadow nods. "What happened after you and Adam formed your resistance?" asks Shadow.

"Well as the fighting continued we gained more and more followers. Both sides were getting desperate and started generating new forms of weapons to fight both of their enemies. This included artificial skills made with magic and placed on strange scrolls for convenience. Surgically altering the devil and angels into living weapons though labeled as super soldiers. Altering some into essentially guardians to take our place as an army of one. As well as altering others into new creatures known as reapers to destroy the souls of their enemies to reduce their numbers and take the souls of humans to increase their own numbers. Supposedly they were based on rumors of creatures that could do those, but naturally and not artificially. Though personally I'm not sure if they were actually real or just rumors. Speaking of which there were even rumors of special weapons that were more powerful than any other seen being developed. Thankfully though they never saw battle," says Eve.

Shadow crosses his arms and starts trembling while gripping his own arms out of fear after hearing that. "I can't believe that they were so insane, Master. How could they let things get that out of hand?" asks Shadow.

"Simple, they were desperate to win and the point of why they started fighting in the first place was already forgotten. All that they cared about at that point was just destroying their enemies. To them nothing else mattered and the battles became more dangerous not to only hell and heaven, but also on earth as well. All three lands were being scarred by all the fighting," says Eve.

"How did you and Adam ever stop the fighting, Master?" asks Shadow, still trembling.

"That was thanks to two small children that wanted to stop the fighting more than even me," says Eve.

Shadow stops trembling and looks at her with his head tilted in confusion. "How did two kids help you stop Armageddon?" asks Shadow.

"They weren't just ordinary children. They were children created from the leftover energy when the hell and heaven realms merged and they gained sentience. This apparently gave them powers greater than anyone could imagine," says Eve.

Shadow tilts his head in confusion. "Wait, so energy from merging realms created living beings with great power. Uhhh, even though there are plenty of stories of gods and goddesses with strange origins this one feels a little out there Master, no offense," says Shadow.

"None taken Shadow. Personally, even now I'm still not sure if they were just making that part up or not. Though one thing that wasn't made up was their incredible power. The merged rulers of hell and heaven recognized their power when they found them and adopted them thinking they could be of use for their respective side. This was probably mainly due to them being more powerful than them and the rulers wanted to have them under their thumbs as quickly as possible. Though neither ruler seemed to be a good parent. Both were neglected in some way while one was always in a state of despair the other was optimistic. By some chance they met each other and became friends. After hearing about the resistance they sought us out. At first most didn't trust them due to their relations to the leaders of the hell and heaven armies. Though Adam and I could tell that they were honest about wanting to end all of the pointless fighting," says Eve.

"How could you and Adam tell that, Master?" asks Shadow.

"It was this gut feeling that the both of us had. After all the fighting I started trusting our gut feelings for decisions like these. They usually paid off in the end and this situation was no different. Due to them being remnant energy of the merged realms they had a surprising amount of knowledge. They knew a way to take away all of the power from the two merged leaders. Which was a good thing because they were the main driving forces of all the fighting. Take them out and most if not all fighting would end. After finding and reaching the only place in hell with both demonic and angelic energy flowing through it they began carving a seal on the ground. Adam, Kaas, Simon, and myself also helped while following their instructions to get it done faster before being spotted. After it was done the ground with the seal rose up into the air, creating a large hill. This was quickly noticed by both sides and the leaders were informed that their adopted children were not only with the child of the enemy, but also the leader and high-ranked members of the resistance. Both leaders rushed to us, which was exactly what we wanted. When they got close enough the two children performed the spell. By the time they finished the leaders were within the seal radius, which was what we wanted. At that time the seal glowed and a light started shining. A red and white pillar of light came from the seal. With the two rulers now trapped they started screaming in pain. The seal was separating the merged rulers into multiple beings again, but not into the original gods that created them. When the seal stopped glowing the merged rulers were nothing but dried husks and seventeen new beings were standing around them. These were the seven sins and the Ten Commandments. Then in a matter of seconds all fighting stopped and armageddon was declared to be over. With all of us happy to hear that it was over it was quickly disrupted with a loud scream from one of the kids. It seems that while everyone was distracted one of the children was killed. At first we thought they died from overexertion from performing the spell, but I quickly saw that they had been shot from behind. It's hard to say who did it or if it was truly intended for them or not. Before any of us could figure out how it happened both of them started glowing, then just disappeared. Needless to say everyone was confused. While we were trying to figure out what happened the appointed leaders of the sins and commandments, Sloth, and one of the commandments performed some kind of reincarnation spell on the two of them. With the knowledge that the two would come back the sins and commandments returned to clearing out the battlefields. Hell's soldiers dispersed and heaven's soldiers left for their realm. With all of them leaving, the commandments told Adam, Simon, and others of the resistance that originated from heaven that they must also return. When Adam asked if he could stay in hell or if I could go back with him they all declined. Their reason was that we were seen as a key to keeping the two realms peaceful. We argued against them, but to no avail. Which sucked because we argued with them for several hours. In the end they gave us titles and land as compensation as part of the original deal that was struck near the beginning of the original war. We really didn't want them, but they were forced onto us. Personally I think they did it so they could keep an eye on us. After that the commandments took Adam and the rest of the heaven bound resistance members as well as the husk of the merged heavenly god the commandments spawned from. The sins also took hell's merged god husk and sealed him in his castle, then each sin took a piece of it and turned it into their own palace. I assume the commandments did the same back in heaven. With that the story comes to an end. Do you have any more questions, Shadow?" says Eve, giving a loud yawn.

"A couple come to mind, Master. Though maybe I should wait till later," says Shadow, not wanting to keep his master up.

Eve smiles at Shadow, seeing that he's concerned for her. "Ok, we can pick this up in the morning. We'll have plenty of time on the walk out anyway. You should also rest yourself because it's going to be a long day for you tomorrow," says Eve, getting up from the chair. When Eve is close to the door she then notices that she left the book on the chair. "You could look through that if you want before going back to bed," says Eve, leaving through the door.

After that Shadow picks up the book and flips through it and notices all of the former students that she had. Through those pictures Shadow noticed something strange about Eve. It seems that her skin, hair, and eyes were different colors. Even though she looked completely different, Shadow was able to recognize her. Shadow just shrugged it off and decided that he could ask her about it tomorrow. With that, Shadow places the book back down and heads back to his room to get some more sleep. When he gets back to his room he removes his mask and goes back to bed.

The Journey Begins

After a couple of hours of going back and forth between being asleep and being awake just lying in bed waiting for morning Shadow decides to just get up and get ready. Shadow puts his mask back on and gets out of bed. Shadow then starts looking around the room for his bag of belongings when he notices that his bag was missing. Shadow is confused and starts to have a mini panic attack wondering where it is. Suddenly a knock comes from the door to the room. When Shadow opens the door Eve is standing there with his bag in hand. "Here, while we were talking last night I had Medea snag your bag to have it washed. I wanted to make sure you started your journey fresh," says Eve, handing the bag back to Shadow.

Shadow takes the bag from Eve and notices that even the bag itself has been cleaned. "Thank you so much Master, you really didn't have to do this for me, But I do really appreciate it," says Shadow, choking up a little.

Eve notices Shadow choking up over this, which to her isn't much of a big deal. "Don't worry about it so much, Shadow. I'm the mother of humanity so my motherly instincts wanted me to make sure you were all set before you left. Now come on, get changed and come down, I already have breakfast ready," says Eve.

Eve closes the door to give Shadow some privacy. Shadow quickly gets changed into a long-sleeved shirt, a pair of jeans, a pair of gloves, a set of socks and shoes, and a mask to cover his face, all of which are the color black. Lastly he dawns the cloak that Eve gave him yesterday. Shadow then tries out the cloak's storage spell by placing his bag into it. With that, Shadow walks down to the kitchen where Eve is already eating. Without thinking Shadow grabs a plate and cup without even looking at what is on and in them. He picks them up as if he's going to move them. Eve notices this just before taking another bite of her food and knows what he's trying to do. "Shadow, you're doing it again. I keep telling you that you can eat at the table," says Eve.

Shadow quickly realizes what he's doing and places everything back down. "Sorry Master, my muscle memory acted before I could think. I'm just used to eating my meals on the floor," says Shadow in an embarrassed tone.

Eve simply scratches her head. She understands what Shadow means since she also has habits that she does solely by muscle memory. However she's also somewhat annoyed because this is the tenth time this has happened. "It's ok this time Shadow, but you need to be more careful about it when you're out there. You need to be able to catch this yourself," says Eve.

Shadow nods and sits down at the table and quickly consumes the breakfast prepared for him, which consists of a few eggs, a couple slices of toast, and a cup of lukewarm coffee. Eve pauses from eating and points to Shadow's drink. "I had your drink sit out to cool off since I don't have any ice. I know that you don't like hot coffee," says Eve.

"Thank you so much Master. As long as it's not hot it's fine. Thank you for taking the time to make me a cup and putting it out to cool. Also again thank you for cleaning my belongings before I left Master," says Shadow, bowing slightly while still sitting. *It's more effort than most people would do for me*, thinks Shadow, finishing his food.

Eve is a little concerned about Shadow thanking her three times for something that to her isn't even that big of a deal. "I mean I appreciate all the thanks, but I feel like you are making a bigger deal out of something small. Also try not to eat so fast, you'll give yourself a stomach cramp. I know you told me you're used to it, but I can't help but feel concerned," says Eve.

Shadow looks down, away from Eve and at his empty plate. "I'm sorry Master, I'll try to slow down," says Shadow, getting up to clean his plate and cup.

Eve finishes up herself, with Shadow taking her dishes and cleaning them as well before she can even say anything. Eve doesn't mind, but is worried that someone might take advantage of his need to be of use to others. After Shadow finishes the dishes he sees Eve at the door with what seems to be a lantern, waiting for him. Shadow and Eve exit her home and get to the entrance of the cave her home resides in. The cave itself is a giant maze that someone could easily get lost in. It doesn't help that the only light available to them comes from both the light outside Eve's home and the lantern that Eve is carrying. While walking through the maze Shadow stays close to Eve less for light, but more to not get lost since he couldn't see when he came through the first time.

To liven up the walk Eve decides to talk about something. "Well since we have some time you said you had a couple of questions about the story from last night, right? What were they?" asks Eve.

"Oh ok, well what happened to everyone afterward? Also how did Armageddon change lives here after it was over? If you don't mind me asking, Master," says Shadow.

Eve scratches the side of her head, thinking about it, having known Shadow would have questions about that. "Well for the first question, when it comes to most of our soldiers I have little to no idea what happened to them. I assume they just went back to their daily lives. Kaas however gained a skill that extended his life span, which he used to continue to hone his blacksmithing. Nowadays anything he makes is considered high quality. Most devils will just buy something if it just has his name attached to it regardless of what it is. As for Simon he was promoted to a domination. Supposedly he became a trusted right hand of the commandments and has been tasked with moving between hell and heaven to relay messages between them and the sins, something that seems beneath him, but he is the only one seemingly trusted enough to handle it. Also when he does this he returns to his former more humanlike archangel form, mainly just to not draw as much attention. When he occasionally finds me we talk to catch up. Though it's mainly just him bragging about his position. Sadly I know the least about Adam. Simon isn't even sure about him, just that he's living in seclusion, probably for the same reason I do. As for myself I received the title of duchess and the land I was given had a mansion on it. I'm unsure whether it was already there or built for me and at the same time I don't really care. All that mattered was that it was a place to live. Though soon enough arrogant devils would come by to challenge me, thinking that beating me would prove their might. After only two weeks of that I left and went to find a new home away from all of them. When I found this cave I started making what eventually became all of this. Though it didn't take long for Sloth to find me and question what I was doing. After explaining the situation we came to an agreement that she won't reveal my new home on the condition that I don't get involved in their problems. Unless all of hell is in trouble. Which was fine by me.

"As for your second question. With all the underworld realms merged things were in great disarray in the beginning. Landmarks and settlements were moved, destroyed, and/or changed due to the merge. Unorganized chaos was happening also because of the realms merging, but also because of armageddon, and the rulers merging into one. Though after the sins and commandments were created, 'order' returned here. Hell was divided up between the sins. They quelled all the devils and demons. Most of those classified as monsters were also brought down to also help quell the chaos on earth that came from armageddon. New towns and cities were formed and some already existing villages and towns were placed under the control of that territory's sin. The parts of the castle that the sins took to live in and rule from have now become landmarks and the location of the largest city in each territory. Lastly that hill that was created from the spell that created the sins and commandments has become a sacred place. There have been columns and altars at several points of it making a star-like shape. It's mainly used for traveling between the three realms. You may not remember since you were blinded at the time but that's where I found you. You're lucky that I passed by there by chance," says Eve.

"Yes, and I'll be forever grateful for that and everything else that you've done for me," says Shadow.

"Oh, some other things that came from armageddon are still around to this day for better or worse!" exclaims Eve.

"What are they Master?" asks Shadow.

"Well those skill scrolls for one. They can be bought in shops and have made things easier around here. They're still mainly used by the warriors of this era, though I guess they're called hunters now. Well either way they're just as useful now as they were back then. On the other hand however those stupid fucking slave masks are also still around and being used. Though their use is restricted and mostly monitored. The reapers and super warriors, at least the devil ones, are still around," says Eve.

"Really? What happened to them?" asks Shadow.

"Well the reapers mainly either work those with titles or under the sins. The super warriors however are just scattered around hell waiting for an opponent, but they shouldn't bother you if you don't bother them. Oh, looks like we're getting close to the entrance," says Eve.

Soon enough the light from the entrance of the cave is visible. Eve turns off her lantern as they get closer to the entrance. At the entrance there is a forest of dead-looking trees made of obsidian. They look like they are growing from the ground which has a deep crimson color like bedrock and produces heat that you can even feel through your shoes. When you expect the scent of sulfur the only scent around comes from the sulfur mixed with the obsidian and bedrock. It's unclear if Eve carved and/or placed these "trees" here or if they were already here when she got here. The same can be said about the cave where her home resides. There is a giant fireball far above them in place of the sun to indicate it being daytime in hell.

As soon as they get outside Eve can sense that something wasn't normal, but decides to not say anything about it so Shadow won't worry about it.

"Shadow, look over at me real quick. I want to see if you can see it now that we are out of my home," Eve says.

Shadow looks over at Eve and can immediately see a multicolored smoke-like cloud around his master. "I can see you surrounded by a colorful cloud. Is this the aura that you told me about Master?" asks Shadow.

"Yes it is and it seems like your new eyes are doing what they are supposed to do. This should give you an edge down here. Though that will take some time since I can tell you are having to focus to see the auras. Don't worry, soon enough it will become second nature to you. Soon not just the sins, but also other devils, monsters, and demons will become easier to deal with. Since you can see their auras now it will be harder for them to sneak up on you and you will be able to judge how strong they are and how they will fight you. Though most demons will leave you alone if you leave them alone unless they are on a hunt and see you as prey. Any demons that do try to fight I would suggest that you kill them because the meat of most of them tastes great once cooked," explains Eve. Eve then points to a devil-made trail a ways off from them through the trees.

"Just follow the trail and you will find the cities the sins control. Just be sure to stay on it as long as you can. It's both the quickest and coolest way to get to the sins. Though I suggest that you don't take on the closest sin from here," says Eve.

"Why is that, Master? Is there something wrong with that city?" asks Shadow.

"Not any more than the others, but I think the sin in control of that one is Pride. That one might be a little too strong for you to go against right now," explains Eve.

So as usual I'm just not good enough, thinks Shadow.

"I suggest that you go for Envy or Lust to start off with," says Eve.

"Why should I start with those sins, Master?" asks Shadow.

"To my knowledge those sins will be the weakest ones of the seven and the closest one to us is Lust, just past Pride. You can tell the strength of the sin's control of the city based on its base," explains Eve.

"How can I tell that, Master?" asks Shadow.

"Simple, their bases resemble chess pieces from earth and the piece their base resembles represents their strength," explains Eve.

"Oh alright. Wait what?" asks Shadow surprisingly. He immediately looks at his master to see if she's being serious.

Eve looks at Shadow, who is confused at her explanation. "Don't worry about it for now, just head to Envy's or Lust's cities," says Eve.

Fine, at least I'll know it's the base when I see it, thinks Shadow. Shadow refocuses. "So where is that sin's base?" asks Shadow.

Eve points to the side of the trail heading east. "After crossing the bridge to exit Pride's territory it should roughly take you four days on foot to get to Lust's city and another two or three to Envy's. Thankfully these three territories are relatively small compared to the others. Though some time ago I heard that there's a faster way to their cities, but I never heard how exactly, so you may want to look into it. You will end up passing through Pride's territory, but if you cause them no trouble on the way they won't bother you. You should be able to reach the city that Pride's base is in by the end of the day at the latest. In fact you might want to stop in Pride's city to rest and grab a weapon as well as some heat-resistant boots because your shoes will not last all the way to Lust's territory. It would also be good to grab any other supplies you believe you'll need for your journey. While you're there you might even find the new kind of transportation they have that can get you to Lust's territory faster," explains Eve.

"Alright I should leave now then while the 'sun' or whatever that thing is is still up," says Shadow.

Shadow starts making his way to the trail, but Eve holds him back. "Hold on just a second Shadow. Here, take this," says Eve. Eve hands him a small sack.

Shadow opens it and sees that it's filled with coins, each with a gem in the middle, as well as what looks like an egg-shaped rock.

"It would be wise to buy a sword in Pride's city while on the way. What you can get with that probably won't be great, but it will be far better than my training swords. Since you're not used to the currency down here I put in a little cheat sheet in there as well to help," says Eve.

Shadow pulls out the stone from the sack and looks at it with confusion. All of a sudden the stone shines slightly, confusing Shadow more. "Oh don't worry about that, for now just keep it with you at all times. I have a feeling it will be of use to you when the time comes," says Eve.

Shadow nods and places the egg back into the sack and puts it into his cloak.

"Oh and also take this. It has some food for you while you're on your way there because it's going to be a long trip to the nearest city," says Eve, handing Shadow the box of food.

"Thank you so much Master," says Shadow. *Geez, I didn't even think about either of those. I hope Master didn't have to scrounge around for it to make up for my stupidity,* thinks Shadow.

"Well this is as much as I can do for you. I can't join you since I have a nonaggression pact with the sins. If I got personally involved things would get far more hectic and make it more difficult to achieve your goal," says Eve, apologizing to Shadow.

"No you've already done more for me than most would care to. Thank you for everything Master, goodbye for now," says Shadow.

As Shadow walks towards the trail, Eve says, "I know you will succeed, Shadow. Have confidence in yourself."

Shadow hesitates for a moment, then gives a shaky, pathetic thumbs-up to Eve without looking at her as he reaches the trail.

Damn it, that's just sad. You're not fooling me with that thumbs-up. You're my student, so have some confidence, thinks Eve.

As soon as he reaches it Shadow starts walking down the part of the trail heading east. Eve watches him walk down the trail. While seeing him off, Eve squats down and picks up a rock from the ground before standing back up. Soon enough Eve can barely see Shadow. She turns her head to the opposite direction to see what looks like a bird. The bird is roughly the size of a crow. It has deep black feathers on its wings with scales of the same color covering the rest of it. Its eyes are the only part that's a different color. They are a bright mirrorlike white. Eve knows that birds with eyes like that are used for spying. She keeps her eyes on it to watch its movements. She isn't yet sure if it's for her or Shadow. Soon enough she sees it start moving its wings to get ready to fly, at which point she chucks the rock at one of the trees. The rock moves through the air with incredible speed, aimed at the birdlike demon perched in one of the trees. The rock makes contact faster than the demon can respond and causes the demon to start bleeding.

"KRAAAAAAA!" says the bird in pain.

The bird starts to jitter around on the branch. Its body begins contorting in unnatural ways. The sound of bones snapping can be heard as it changes shape. The bird also starts growing in size. When it's finished the bird is now around twice its size. There are more scales now covering it. Its wings' skeletal structure is now visible, with only a layer of feathers covering each bone. The eyes now possess bright piercing-red pupils staring at Eve.

That thing was spying on us as soon as we came out of my home. Why? It can also take a hit like that and still be alive. That's no normal demon, thinks Eve while trying to grab more rocks.

While bending down to look for another rock to throw Eve keeps her eyes focused on the demon. Though before she has the chance the demon lets out a loud cry, showing its mouth is filled with sharp canine teeth. Eve gets ready for it to come at her, but instead it flies away. It flies west while leaving a slight blood trail.

At least it's going the opposite direction as Shadow, but that demon and whoever is controlling it has me worried. Speaking of being worried, I'm sure he felt me throw that rock. I just hope he doesn't start racking his brain too much and thinking he should come back to check on me. I'm sure he will, but I'm sure he'll know it's better to just keep going to the sins, thinks Eve as she goes back into her cave.

Route to the Sins

Shadow reaches the edge of the trees, but starts to worry. Both for the journey ahead and for his master. He could feel a strange presence watching them. He even felt a slight shock wave that came from where his master was. Still standing at the edge, he feels unable to move. He starts debating whether he should head back or not to make sure she's alright. *Should I go back? No, Master Eve can handle this. Then again, what if that weird presence is really strong? No, she'll be fine on her own. If I go back she'll probably just scold me. I should just keep moving forward, otherwise I'll never rescue them,* thinks Shadow. With his inner debate finished he starts walking down the trail again.

It has been several hours since Shadow started walking. Shadow is far into Pride's territory and is heading towards Pride's city to get equipment, then head off to the sins that Eve told him to start off with. However, the heat continually increases as time goes on and shows no sign of slowing down. Even the air is so hot now that even breathing is a bit painful. Even when he does breathe the only thing that he smells is sulfur and his shoes melting. Though he knows stopping or turning back aren't much of a set of options at this point, so he continues to walk down the trail. As he walks the only things he sees are mostly flat land with some large rocks here and there, and some ruins of what looks like a village or town with the remains of their structures barely standing, showing they've been abandoned for quite some time. When looking at some of the ruins Shadow can tell that some parts of the ruins look relatively newer than other parts. He concludes that the parts that look newer are the inner parts that were exposed when the buildings were destroyed. From his best guess he concludes that they were destroyed around maybe one to two decades ago. *These people, or I guess I should say devils, just wanted to live somewhere peacefully. I wonder who or what left this town in such a destroyed state? Either way I hope that they all got away safely at least,* thinks Shadow. He quickly steps onto a piece of rubble and places his hands together to give a little prayer to those that probably died.

Shadow continues walking down the trail and observes more around him to keep himself alert of any potential dangers. Sometimes he passes by what looks like a shrub or tree though they don't look very healthy. It seems that any plant life visible along the trail is mostly if not completely dead. It's a clear departure from where he is from on earth or even Eve's home.

The farther away he gets from the "forest" near Eve's home the more the dominant the scent of sulfur becomes. The heat also does become more apparent, especially on the ground. The heat is bad enough that Shadow can feel it through his shoes and can tell that they are slowly melting. The only things that can be heard are the steps of his feet, the movement of his clothes, and a faint scream in the distance. He's unaware of where it's coming from. At times like this, being alone with one's thoughts could either be a good or bad thing.

Am I sure that I can really do this? I've been trained so I should be fine. Though I don't know how strong anything around here is and I don't have a sword. All the more reason to get to Pride's city as quickly as possible. Hopefully I don't run into anything or anyone really dangerous along the way. Well I have already made it this far so I should be fine. Then again the danger might be waiting to ambush me just before the city. That shouldn't be a problem, they probably won't attack me. Yeah, I don't really look like I have anything of value. Though that hasn't stopped others before. NO, stop thinking like that. I just need to get to the city, get a sword, and get some new shoes since mine definitely aren't made for long walks in hell. If I do that I should be fine... maybe, thinks Shadow, arguing with himself.

As he continues walking he eventually starts seeing some occasional demons roaming around, but since Shadow leaves them alone they leave him alone, just as Eve said. Eventually, one does stop in front of him to pick a fight. The demon appears to be a grayish orthrus, but something about it seems a little off. The two heads look different. The left head resembles a Red Heeler, but he isn't sure what the right head is. He sighs, slightly feeling like he jinxed himself. He can see its aura and that it's large and vicious. Wanting to avoid the confrontation entirely, he tries to move to the side slowly to let it pass. However, the two heads follow his movements.

"RUFF," says the left head.

"Ruff," says the right head.

Suddenly something clicks with Shadow as he figures out why the demon feels off. "Ah, one of the heads is a dog or wolf and the other is a fox," mumbles Shadow.

The right head suddenly lowers itself. It seems upset by Shadow pointing out it's a fox. The left head starts nudging the other to try and cheer it up. Their aura now looks deflated, especially around the right head.

Shadow sees this and tilts his head slightly in confusion. "Huh, why is it feeling depressed? Does it have a complex about being a fox instead of a dog? If so then I don't see why. Foxes are cool and it doesn't seem like something to be depressed about. If anything, the fact that they're a dog and fox head makes them seem more unique and interesting," mutters Shadow.

The two heads hear him and perk up immediately. They look at Shadow with joyful eyes. It seems that was the first time anyone complimented them. Their aura grows again, but it now has a joyful feel around it. It begins nuzzling its heads against him. Shadow responds to this by petting the two heads. However, the happy moment quickly drops when the scent of Shadow's shoes that are starting to melt wafts around them. Without hesitation the fox head grabs Shadow with its teeth and puts him on its back.

"Oh thank you very much for that. I guess it was getting too hot for my shoes to handle," says Shadow.

"WOOF," says the left head.

"Woof," says the right head.

It really is nice in the end. Maybe it acted mean because of its complex. It probably doesn't run into many that appreciate it for who it is. I can understand that all too well. It's better for screwups and outcasts like us to stick together. Hm, while I'm on them now I should check to see how bad my shoes melted, thinks Shadow.

Shadow decides to look at his left leg to check the damage to his shoe. The shoe seems to only be slightly melted. He calculates that at the rate he's been going he wouldn't have made it to the city before his shoes fully melted and he would be walking basically barefoot.

Suddenly the orthrus starts turning and begins walking down the trail in the direction towards Pride's city.

"Huh, are you taking me down the trail so I burn myself?" asks Shadow.

"WOOF," says the left head.

"Woof," says the right head.

"Ah, what good boys you both are," says Shadow as he pets both heads as best as he can.

As they continue down the trail Shadow notices that his hands and parts of his clothes seem to be covered in ash or dust. He wonders about it for a second, then sees the parts where he petted them and sees that the fur is now whiter. Curious, he pets another area and finds that their fur isn't actually gray, but white with some brown spots.

Huh, I guess it hasn't been able to clean its fur so the ash and/or dust must have just collected on its fur. Wait, is there even a place in hell where it can clean this off? Well I guess it doesn't really matter either way. The orthrus doesn't seem to mind it as far as I can tell. Hm, just referring to it as 'the orthrus' seems kind of impersonal. What if we run into another one? That'll make it more difficult to refer to it. Maybe I should come up with a name to call it. Let's see, what would be a good name? Geez, I was never good at coming up with names back on earth. Hmm, ok I think I got one. Now let's see if it likes it, thinks Shadow.

"Uh hey would you mind if I gave you a name to call you?" asks Shadow.

"WOOF," says the left head joyfully.

"Woof," says the right head joyfully.

Its aura grows with joy and anticipation at the concept of receiving a name.

"Ok I'll take that as a yes. Well how do you feel about the name 'Tai'?" asks Shadow.

The orthrus stops and the two heads look at each other. They think it over for a few seconds. Shadow becomes worried that they don't like it. Suddenly the orthrus starts jumping with joy. Shadow does everything he can to keep from falling off.

"Well I guess you like the name then huh?" asks Shadow.

The orthrus stops jumping and the two heads look at Shadow.

"WOOF," says the left head joyfully.

"Woof," says the right head joyfully.

"Ok, then from now on you are Tai the orthrus," declares Shadow.

Tai begins jumping with joy again. Then after a couple of jumps he starts running down the trail faster than before. They speed past other demons, but most either continue to ignore them or are too slow to do anything to them. Shadow again does everything he can to keep from falling off. Tai out of nowhere makes a sudden stop which would've sent Shadow flying if he wasn't holding onto him so tightly, though he does hit his head a little against Tai's back. Shadow starts to reorient himself while rubbing his head and seeing why Tai stopped. Just their luck, they are surrounded by a pack of more orthruses.

Ah fuck, more of them. Was this just a setup and Tai plans to betray me? Was that his plan all along? No, looking more closely at their behavior it's clear that they don't care for him and are looking at us with disgust. I guess his appearance is too unsightly to them. Probably using me as a bargaining chip won't change that. That would explain why he was so happy when I complimented him if this is what he had to deal with. Hmm, now that I think about it I wonder if this is the pack that Tai is from. If it is then this might be good and they'll just let us pass, but something tells me that they most likely won't. This could most likely just end in a fight if I'm not careful, thinks Shadow.

The leader of the pack steps forward. He has several scars all over his body ranging in sizes, though it's far less than other members of the pack that have more than double the scars then him. Yet the others of the pack listen to his commands. He stares down the two and intimidates them slightly. It's clear he's not afraid to fight, but is more skilled and/or less reckless than the others of the pack. Both of his heads resemble a German shepherd. These already put Shadow into a nervous state. The leader starts circling Tai and Shadow. They start getting more nervous about this. As the leader returns to where he started he looks at Tai straight in the eyes.

"RUUFFF," says the leader's two heads.

Suddenly the other orthruses begin moving. They surround them in a more organized way. The area now resembles a makeshift arena with the orthruses surrounding them being the border. Their aura is now more condensed and forms a wall higher than several stories. It seems that the leader wants to fight Tai one-on-one and makes sure that escape is next to impossible.

Crap, what do we do now? He clearly wants to fight, but this could be a lose-lose situation. If we lose then the outcome might most likely be death. If we win then the others might just jump us all at once for a chance at dominance. Either scenario is made worse since I still have no weapon to fight with, limiting my abilities. Currently I'm more or less just going to be dead weight to Tai, though I'm used to being seen as dead weight. I need to think of some way to both help Tai win and get both of us out of here in one piece, thinks Shadow.

Tai takes a stance showing both sets of teeth. The leader however isn't doing the same. He seems partially paralyzed. He is just eyeing Tai, almost looking past him. Neither choosing to make the first move.

"RUFF," says the leader orthrus.

Two of the orthruses start moving from their position. This in turn makes an opening to leave from. For a second Shadow is both confused and hopeful that they are letting them go, though he quickly changes that thought, knowing it won't be that easy. He feels that Tai feels the same since he hasn't moved even slightly. Just as he comes to that conclusion, an orthrus, almost twice the size of not only the leader and Tai but all of the other orthrus, walks through the opening. This orthrus has light brown fur and is covered in scars, more than double the leader's. Its heads resemble a Tibetan Mastiff. Needless to say both Shadow and Tai are nervous beyond belief. After the giant orthrus fully walks through the opening the other orthrus that are making, they immediately move back into position. He walks up to the leader and bows. The bow looks like it's being done a bit begrudgingly, but he bows all the same. He now stands next to the leader, making his size more noticeable.

So he's going to test us. Though something feels off about the relationship between those two. I get the feeling that giant orthrus used to be the leader. He must've lost to their new leader and became obedient to him whether he likes it or not. Their current leader must be smarter than the rest and thinks the situations through. Well hopefully that's the case. If so then maybe we can outsmart this giant, thinks Shadow.

Shadow eyes the giant orthrus, trying to find a weakness Tai can take advantage of. He sees that one of the orthrus's back legs looks slightly weaker than the rest. He concludes that it could be from a former injury that didn't fully heal. Seeing this he climbs up slightly to Tai's heads to tell him of his strategy.

"Ok, it seems like his back right leg is weaker than the rest. If we do have to fight him, aim for that. Afterwards when he's down we can get onto his back and take him down with ease," whispers Shadow, hoping the other orthruses don't hear him.

Tai nods slightly while not taking their eyes off the giant orthrus. They see the leg in question and prepare to charge for it when the signal is given.

"RUFF," says the leader.

Immediately Tai runs over to the bad leg. The giant orthrus at first doesn't understand what Tai is doing. He prepares to take Tai head on. He dives his head to try and bite down on Tai and Shadow. However thanks to Tai's smaller size he is able to just avoid the attack, which was close enough that he could smell his breath, and keep moving. As soon as Tai passes by him the giant orthrus quickly figures out his plan, almost like it's happened before. He tries to move his body out of the way of Tai's path. His bad leg begins lifting off the ground, but it's in vain. Tai bites down on the leg with both heads. His added weight forces the leg back down. Now with it back on the ground and being attacked by Tai the leg gives out. The back of the giant orthrus starts to collapse. While Tai is too focused on aiming at the leg he doesn't see that they're about to be sat upon, but Shadow notices. He quickly pats Tai's necks to get their attention.

"Tai, let go of the leg quickly. Now let's take advantage of the situation and end this," says Shadow.

Tai quickly lets go of the leg and jumps out of the way of the falling back end of the giant orthrus. Now with the giant orthrus basically sitting their back makes a straight shot to the heads. Shadow points towards the back and Tai understands and starts running. Shadow figures that they'll only have a few seconds before their opponent gets back up. Sure enough Shadow is right. The giant orthrus starts moving back up albeit a bit slowly. It's just enough time for Tai to get on top of the back and reach the necks before the giant orthrus can fully stand back up. Now at the necks Shadow doesn't even need to say or do anything. Tai instinctively bites onto the necks of the giant orthrus before they can even shake the two of them off. Immediately after biting down the giant orthrus does everything to shake them off, but to no avail. Tai only bites down harder and Shadow holds onto Tai with everything he has. Even with Tai biting down so hard on his neck the giant orthrus doesn't cry out in pain.

"RUFF," says the leader orthrus suddenly.

Both Tai and the giant orthrus stop what they were doing. Tai jumps off of the giant orthrus's back and Shadow lightens his grip.

I guess the match is over now. The only question is will our results from it be good or bad? thinks Shadow.

The leader orthrus motions their heads behind him. The giant orthrus walks over and sits behind the leader. Now the leader starts circling around Tai and Shadow again. Eyeing the two of them. This obviously makes the two of them nervous. After a few circles the leader stops in front of them.

"Hey be careful, I feel like he's about to try something," whispers Shadow, with Tai nodding.

Then suddenly the leader lunges at them. His left head goes for Tai's right fox head. The two heads start biting at each other. Meanwhile the leader's right head goes not for Tai's other head, but towards Shadow. He sees this and in mere moments he gets to his feet and grabs the leader's head coming at him as best as he can to stop the attack. Tai's left head starts biting one of the leader's necks to get his attention. This does. However, the leader takes his front right paw and starts clawing at Tai's left head. One of the hits cuts around Tai's left eye. The pain is enough for Tai's left head to release his grip on the leader's right neck. Now the leader can move a bit closer to his target. Shadow sees this and becomes enraged.

Without much thought Shadow just starts punching the sharp canine tooth he can see in the leader's mouth. After several punches the tooth rips out of the mouth with Shadow grabbing it immediately. He pulls himself onto the snout of the leader's right head and starts stabbing it with the tooth he ripped out. Shadow knows that this might not do much, but it's the best he can do in this situation.

Suddenly the leader orthrus stops moving. This catches the two of them by surprise. Confused, Tai tries to back away to try and get some distance when the leader just disappears. Shadow falls back onto Tai's back while trying to make sure not to hit him with the tooth still in his hand. Now even more confused, the two take a few seconds to look around them to see where the leader went. They look in front of them and the leader is back where he was before he started circling the two of them.

So he was holding back on us. So he really was just testing us. If he took us seriously then we never would've stood a chance. Even if we ran away he could have cut us off easily, thinks Shadow with great doubt in mainly his own abilities.

"RUFF," says the leader orthrus.

The others of the pack start moving. They open a path in the direction the two of them were heading before they were trapped.

Is... is he letting us go? Did Tai's abilities show them that he's worthy of respect and are letting us go? Then again they might think that he's too weak and not worth bothering with. If so then it must be my fault. I told him what he should've done in the first battle. The leader did try to attack me. Maybe having a rider is seen as a sign of weakness. Maybe the path is just for me and they want Tai to abandon me so he can stay. If so then that's fine, it's not like it's the first time. He's helped me more than he probably should have anyways. I can make the rest of the way myself. I should return the leader's tooth as an apology for knocking it out earlier, thinks Shadow as he starts to dismount Tai.

Tai however begins walking, making it difficult for Shadow to try and dismount. Shadow is confused by this and wonders what Tai is doing. As the two pass the leader Tai only nods to him and continues walking. As soon as Tai passes what was the border of the makeshift arena the pack begins walking in the opposite direction. Shadow is just left so confused by what just happened that he forgot to offer the tooth back to the leader. He just puts the tooth into his cloak and looks towards Tai's heads.

"Huh, so you're not going with them?" asks Shadow.

Both of Tai's heads turn towards Shadow the best that they can and shake no. This both makes Shadow happy and sad. He's happy because Tai will still be with him, but sad because he thinks that he unintentionally forced him to choose to stay with him. Shadow tries to say something to Tai to confirm his thoughts, but Tai starts running back down the trail. Shadow now has to focus more on staying on than anything else again. Tai runs for several minutes, passing more demons and another set of ruins. Though Shadow doesn't have time to look at them this time since Tai just ran right through them. Suddenly Tai starts slowing down, which confuses Shadow. Have they already made it to Pride's city? Eventually Tai stops altogether. Shadow looks at what's ahead, but it's not the city. Instead he sees what appears to be a fog.

From One Ally to Another

Tai stops just before the fog. It's so dense that they can't see anything immediately past it. It's acting somewhat like a visual curtain. The concept of a fog this dense puzzles Shadow somewhat. With how hot it is currently and with it continually increasing this shouldn't necessarily be possible. Tai sniffs around and doesn't smell any danger but waits to see what Shadow thinks. Shadow starts to contemplate the fog.

Hmm, this doesn't make sense. Normally fog forms when it cools down and causes condensation. If it was in the morning it might be possible, but it should be roughly around mid day by now. Could it be steam that might make more sense? Though I don't hear any kind of liquid steaming so it shouldn't be so dense here. Then again, hell is a different plain of existence. The rules could be different here than back on earth. Actually since this is hell there's no guarantee that steam or fog is necessarily safe. It could be some kind of trap of poisonous gas or another ambush. Though the latter might not be the case. Tai doesn't seem to be reacting to any kind of threat so maybe I'm just overthinking it. Then again what if he does smell something and is waiting on me to pick up on them too? Should we just try to run around it or just run through it and hope for the best? AUGH, thinks Shadow, getting more nervous and paranoid.

After finishing his self-argument Shadow starts noticing that he and Tai are being surrounded by the fog. Shadow notices that it's considerably colder now. He even starts to notice some ice starting to form on the ground. Now in it whether he likes it or not, Shadow chooses to just have Tai sprint at full speed and get out as fast as they can. However something starts happening to Tai. His heads start barking and biting at nothing. He starts jumping erratically, which causes Shadow to fall off. Shadow is confused by what's going on and calls out to Tai to figure out what's wrong.

"TAI, What's happening?! What are you attacking?! There's nothing there... or is there," says Shadow, as Tai starts moving out of Shadow's view.

Soon enough Tai completely disappears from Shadow's view in the fog. Alone again and with his visibility diminished Shadow chooses to just get out of the fog and keep heading to the city, hopeful that he can reunite with Tai on the way. He looks downward and follows the well-traveled trail that he's been using. He also notices that the area feels noticeably cooler than earlier which does feel nice compared to before. However he sees some ice crystals starting to form on his cloak. If he doesn't get out of the fog soon then his body might start to freeze.

He picks up his pace, but after continually walking on the trail as best as he could he starts to hear voices calling out to him. He recognizes the voices of those he knows from earth. This makes him incredibly nervous for several reasons. However he knows he doesn't have the time to think about what's going on. So he places his hands over his ears and starts running. Though the voices are muffled he can still hear them until they suddenly stop. He stops to try and catch his breath though that has become more difficult. Clumps of ice have started to form on his shirt and pants. He isn't sure, but it feels like it's forming on his bare skin as well. While still looking down he sees lines forming out of his shadow in front of him. He looks up to follow the lines and sees three silhouettes of people that he doesn't recognize. Shadow is unsure what is going on, but presumes this is some kind of mirage.

The first silhouette is hard to discern, but he can see they're close to his height and they have something flowing behind them. The way it moves reminds Shadow of sand. The second one resembles a woman that is a bit shorter than him. However she suddenly disappears while being consumed by a green veil. The last one seems to be a man that towers over him and is incredibly muscular. As soon as he looks at the third silhouette a wave of purple aura surrounds him.

"You'll never beat them the way you are now. Maybe I should help you out so you won't die," says a mysterious voice.

Suddenly Shadow feels something hit him in the chest. It feels like getting jabbed in the heart with a needle. Suddenly more illusions start appearing and of people he knows from earth with their voices returning. Not wanting to deal with the illusions anymore he closes his eyes and covers his ears. When the voices disappear for the second time he opens his eyes and sees that the earth silhouettes are gone as well. The three original silhouettes however now resemble what can be best described as dragons and all of them are now towering over him. Even more confused, Shadow knows that even if they aren't real it's probably wise to get away from them as fast as possible before he freezes to death. He immediately looks back down at the trail and starts running. Eventually the noises he hears are getting farther away though he still doesn't raise his head. After a few minutes of running Shadow can see the fog is no longer surrounding him and that the temperature is rising again. As what ice that did form on him and on the environment around him starts to evaporate he can tell that he's fully out of the fog and it's not another illusion. He starts to slow down to collect his thoughts on what just happened.

Just what the hell was that? Why was I hearing the voices of people I knew? Also just who were those people? Why did they turn into dragons? Was it some kind of mirage, a premonition or just some kind of psychological attack? Either way I need to get out of this weird fog before it happens again. I just hope Tai is ok. Hopefully he got out of there already. I know our time together was short, but I hope we meet up again. Hmm, it's rare that I can say, er, think that, thinks Shadow, looking back at the fog.

Now free of the fog Shadow keeps moving to try and get some distance from the fog. While looking ahead he starts to see what looks like some buildings in the distance. He turns around to look at the fog and make sure it's not following him. Thankfully he notices that it's moving away from him. As if it's being carried by an unfelt breeze. He turns back to the buildings and starts contemplating if it's the city or not.

Is that the city, have I reached it already? Tai was moving really fast so it's a possibility. Though something is weird if it is. I'm not seeing a lot of aura coming from it. You'd think a city would be brimming with aura. Well maybe I just still don't have a handle on my eyes' power yet, thinks Shadow.

After seeing the buildings Shadow starts to pick up his pace a little bit. Even if it's not the city he can just climb up to the highest point and look around to see if the city is in sight yet or if he can spot Tai. As he gets closer he notices that the buildings look damaged and abandoned. However, he starts hearing something coming from these ruins as he gets even closer. The sounds coming from them are the sounds of a fight. Then all of a sudden there is an "AAAAAH!"

That sounds like it's coming from a girl. Wait, was that the scream that I've been hearing for a while now? I should go over there to see if someone needs help. Wait, what if it's a setup for an ambush? Well if it's not I feel I will regret not helping, but I should be prepared for a trap, thinks Shadow. Shadow runs to where he heard the scream, prepared in case it could be a trap.

When he gets there he sees a single green-skinned girl being attacked by a group of around thirty red imps being led by a purple imp, all armed with pitchforks. The auras coming from the imps are purple in color, with a small light purple aura surrounding the red imps and a larger violet aura surrounding the leading purple imp. The girl is fighting them off with two daggers and having only slight success due to their great numbers. Shadow notices there are several imps who are already dead, but she's showing signs of being overwhelmed by their great numbers.

The way she's fighting them is bad when dealing with large groups. I guess not everyone knows the right way to deal with them like Master Eve does, thinks Shadow.

As the fight continues the girl starts to show signs of exhaustion.

She needs help. Wait, this could just be a trick to trap and ambush me, thinks Shadow, hesitating to jump in.

The green-skinned girl continues to fight the imps, but one of the red imps comes up from behind, headbutting her and making her lose her grip on her daggers. The daggers go flying over the battlefield from the attack. With her daggers too far away from her for her to reach, the imps attack.

"AAAAAH!" screams the girl.

Dammit, this better not be a trap, thinks Shadow as he jumps into the fight.

He grabs the pitchfork of one of the imps in front of the girl and flings it at one of the ones behind her, taking its pitchfork from it. The imps stop their attack with confusion at what just happened.

The girl looks at Shadow. "Huh?" says the girl.

"Quick, get up and get your weapons," exclaims Shadow. The girl only nods her head and runs to her daggers while Shadow starts killing any imps that chase after her with the pitchfork that he took from the first imp. The girl picks up her daggers and by the time she turns around to fight the imps with Shadow she sees something surprising.

Shadow has already killed the purple imp and is finishing off the last red imp leading them.

"WHAT?! I've been fighting for around ten minutes and could only kill ten yet in just a few seconds he killed thirty of them and is about to finish off a purple one," says the girl with great irritation in her voice.

After she says that, Shadow finishes off the last imp and starts collecting their pitchforks and placing them into his cloak's storage seal. *Compared to the orthruses from earlier, dealing with the imps wasn't too difficult. Granted this time I had a weapon, but that's beside the point. One of the questions now is what do I do with these imps. I'm only putting them in my cloak since it would seem like a waste to just leave them here. I wonder if I can sell these? If I can it will definitely help when picking up equipment in the city. Also should I grab all their bodies too? Maybe there's a butcher there that might buy them. Because there's no way I can eat all of them. Well I've already got that one other demon I killed while walking earlier. So I'll take them just in case. Also that girl, I should check if she's fine and I should be ready if she's going to attack if my guard is down,* thinks Shadow.

While picking up the last of the pitchforks and the imp corpses he notices a pedestal. The pedestal looks completely fine, almost like new, with some shards of amethyst scattered around it along with the pitchforks. *Should I take these too? They might be worth something, but something about them is giving me a bad feeling so it might be better to just leave them where they are. Also how is this pedestal undamaged when this town is in ruins?* thinks Shadow.

While Shadow is picking up the pitchforks and wondering about the pedestal, the girl is walking towards him.

"Thanks, I really needed help with them. I'm glad you showed up when you did. You're really strong to take care of them so quickly," says the girl as she walks toward Shadow.

"Don't mention it, I'm just glad I could help," says Shadow as he turns toward the girl with a pitchfork hidden behind his back in case she attacks.

When the girl gets to Shadow she reaches a hand out with the intent to shake hands. "I'm Lina, what's your name?" asks Lina.

"Shadow," responds Shadow, hesitating at first, then grabbing Lina's hand to shake it. Getting a closer look at her, Lina has long red hair that flows to her waist. Height-wise she comes up just to Shadow's chest. Her eyes are interesting; her right eye is blue and her left eye is yellow. Her attire consists of a pair of beige pants with a large black belt with a blue bandana tied around it. Also on the belt are two jambiya-style daggers, and the rest of the outfit consists of a pink shirt with white at the ends, a pair of slightly armored white arm gloves with a yellow bandana tied around her left forearm, and a pair of tall white boots made to withstand high heat. Her skin does actually have a green tint to it, but after Shadow closes his eyes for a few seconds her skin now seems to be fair and could easily pass for a human. After getting a good look at Lina he also gets the feeling that she looks familiar, but can't put his finger on it, though he ignores that for now.

Hmm, maybe she has trouble releasing her aura, thinks Shadow.

Lina tries to get a look at Shadow's face and jerks back a little in surprise at his mask.

Not surprising that someone doesn't want to be near me, thinks Shadow.

"Oh it's just a mask, sorry, for a second I thought you were one of those demons or monsters that doesn't have a face, like a reaper. Given the area, you possibly being a reaper would have been very fitting, but it was just for a moment. Again, sorry for my reaction, I guess I was still on edge," says Lina, apologizing to Shadow.

Huh, a reaper. Uh, how should I take that? Doesn't matter for now, she seems to be ok, thinks Shadow. "It's fine... I think?" responds Shadow, letting go of her hand.

The two of them start feeling awkward about the situation. Lina also starts feeling a little awful for making the situation awkward by her action and comment.

Lina starts looking around the area, trying to both find something and make the situation less awkward. "Hey did you happen to see a bag while you were fighting those imps?" asks Lina.

Shadow shakes his head since he was too busy fighting the imps to see her bag.

"Where did my bag fly off to? Could you please help me find it? All my stuff's in it," says Lina.

Shadow nods and starts looking around to help find her bag and notices that this place looks like it's been abandoned for some time. While looking he wonders what happened to this place. The buildings look to be made of some kind of wood with a stone foundation to keep them from burning. There are also the remains of several vehicles. A couple of them look like carriages that were pulled by some kind of beast while the others look like they used to move by their own power, but they're too destroyed for him to be sure. Soon enough Shadow sees a satchel lying on the ground near one of the destroyed vehicles and points to it. "Is that it?" asks Shadow.

Lina looks to where he's pointing. "Yeah that's it!" exclaims Lina, happy it was found. Lina picks up the pitchforks of the imps she killed. "Hold on, this will only take a moment." Lina grabs her bag that got tossed in the fight.

While Lina picks up her bag a pendant with what looks like an emerald on it falls from it. Shadow quickly sees a green aura coming from the pendant for a second.

Lina quickly grabs the pendant and puts it back into her bag, almost like she doesn't want Shadow to notice it.

Why is she so worried about me seeing that? It kind of gives me a similar bad feeling like the gem shards near that pedestal. Well she seems fine now so it doesn't matter. Better get going. I should be close to the city, thinks Shadow as he continues walking to Pride's city.

She puts the pitchforks of the imps she killed in her bag as best she can. *I wonder how he was able to store all those pitchforks in his cloak?* thinks Lina.

She looks over at the imps she killed and sees they're already starting to burn to the point of being useless to sell. She ignores them since they would be more trouble than they would be worth. She then turns around to see Shadow walking away.

"HEY WAIT UP!" yells Lina in an irritated tone.

Shadow stops. *Oh no, is she going to try and make me give her more pitchforks from those imps? Or does she want the imp bodies for herself?*

If so, maybe I should just run for it. No, I should at least hear what she wants, thinks Shadow in a somewhat worried tone.

Lina catches up to Shadow. "Geez, could you just wait a minute so I can put my stuff up? You're also heading to Pride's city, aren't you?" asks Lina.

"Yes I am," responds Shadow.

"Great, I know a shop that can buy all our pitchforks. Also there's a butcher somewhere in the city that will be all over those imp corpses that I saw you collect. You will definitely get some good money for your haul, especially for the purple imp's pitchfork," says Lina as the two of them continue walking to the city.

"Are they really worth that much?" asks Shadow.

"Well not the pitchforks themselves, but the material they're made out of is. It acts like a metal, but is made of a demon's condensed aura. Once processed, it helps keep buildings from burning when used as part of its foundation. Though it's hard to get because the demons that create it are aggressive and will attack devils on sight, especially when they're seen alone," explains Lina.

Ok so maybe she finds it safer to be in a group until we get to the city. I should at least let her show me where I can sell this loot. Maybe I can even get a sword there. Though I might ask for directions to the butcher since it doesn't seem she knows exactly where it is in the city, thinks Shadow.

"Oh, you probably shouldn't try to sell the one from the leading imp though. I doubt anyone will believe that the two of us could take it down, let alone just you. Plus it's really dumb to be walking out here without some way to defend yourself," says Lina.

Shadow nods, understanding that it would only make him stand out more than he'd like. Shadow then looks over at Lina, somewhat confused. "Are you out here all by yourself? Were you not with others before we met?" asks Shadow.

Lina stops and starts getting irritated by Shadow's question. "Are you asking if I'm some child that got separated from her family?" asks Lina in a very irritated tone. Her skin starts turning green again with her anger.

Ah crap I think I just stepped on a landmine. Better clear up the misunderstanding or this will end badly for me, thinks Shadow. Due to her physique she could easily be mistaken for being younger than she really is and it's a very sensitive issue for her. "No, I'm just asking since you were fighting those imps by yourself. I was wondering if there were other people that either abandoned you or were killed before we met up. As you said it's not wise to travel out here alone," says Shadow, trying to calm her.

"Oh yes, I was traveling by myself before you showed up to help me. I honestly had little desire to travel with others before. Sorry about that, I thought that you were looking down at me," says Lina.

Lina starts to calm down and her skin changes back to normal. They then continue walking to the city. While walking Shadow notices that they are starting to walk uphill slightly.

"So why are you covering your face?" asks Lina.

Shadow gets slightly depressed and doesn't look over at Lina. "Personal reasons," responds Shadow very uncomfortably.

Lina quickly realizes that she asked something she shouldn't have this time and quickly tries to change the topic to make the walk less awkward. "So how were you able to kill all those imps in just a few seconds? I could barely kill ten in several minutes," says Lina.

"You were making it one versus forty-one. That could get you some kills but their numbers proved too much. I just made it one-on-one thirty-one times. I also targeted their leader first as soon as I could to throw them into a panic. My master told me that's the more efficient way to fight large groups of demons," says Shadow.

"Really? I'll keep that in mind for next time, thanks for the tip. Hey, your master wouldn't happen to be the great warrior Eve, would it?" asks Lina.

Shadow doesn't respond to Lina's question, but she can somehow already tell that Eve was his master.

"I thought so. From my experience a way to tell if someone actually trained under Eve is that they don't want to admit to training under her out of respect, while others just wanting to get attention will exclaim that she trained them when she really didn't. Hm, now that I'm thinking about it, Eve had a similar style of fighting large groups. She also takes on a student every few centuries or so. The style of fighting to take demons out quickly is also like her style as well. Uh, at least that's what I've heard anyways," says Lina. Lina quickly tries to change the subject. "So do you mind if I use what you told me next time I'm in a situation like that?" asks Lina.

Shadow nods to her and then Lina starts to giggle both joyfully and awkwardly.

"By the way, why were so many of them attacking you in the first place?" asks Shadow.

Lina tenses up. "Oh uh, I just happened to be unlucky and got caught in their sights when they were in a large group," responds Lina.

"Oh that's really unfortunate, hopefully that doesn't happen again," says Shadow.

"Eh yeah, I hope that too," says Lina in an awkward tone. *I can't tell him it's because I kept throwing rocks at them and hiding because their reaction was funny and they finally found me. It would be too embarrassing*, thinks Lina.

As they continue walking Lina looks more at Shadow and notices something different about him. "You know you're really different from the normal devils around here. Which territory are you from anyways?" asks Lina.

"Earth," responds Shadow as he sees the city coming closer into view and hears some sounds coming from there.

"Earth, that's neat... WAIT, EARTH?! How can someone from the earth realm be here not as a sinner?" asks Lina.

"It's a personal reason," responds Shadow with slight anger in his voice while clenching his fist.

Lina seems suspicious of Shadow's answer. *That doesn't answer my question. Why and how is an earth-lander here? Did Eve really train an earth-lander? No, I bet he's just a sinner that got away. It happens sometimes and since few are out here these days it's not a bad place to hide. He must have been nearly finished with his sentence since there are no sinful trees coming from his body. He probably wears that mask to hide his roots. He probably also uses it to look like a reaper so people won't bother him. I should try to take it off to check*, thinks Lina. Lina starts reaching for Shadow's mask with one of her hands. Her other hand is reaching for one of her daggers to fight back if he gets hostile.

Shadow sees that she is reaching for him and her weapon. Huh, what's she doing? thinks Shadow.

As soon as Lina touches the mask, Shadow reacts immediately. He grabs the wrist of the hand reaching for his mask. He then places his hand on top of her other hand and holds it down, keeping her unable to pull out her dagger.

"What are you doing?!" asks Shadow in an angered tone.

"Uh, I was curious what a non-sinner earth-lander looked like. Come on, I want to see, please," says Lina, lying about her real intention.

Shadow doesn't let go of her hands, getting more angry. "NO," responds Shadow, tightening his grip.

Lina can feel how angry Shadow is becoming. Lina realizes that she did something she shouldn't have. "I'm sorry, I didn't have any bad intentions about it. It's just that it's rare to see someone from earth in hell that isn't a sinner. Though now I see you don't want your mask removed. So I promise to not try it again. So can you let go of my arms and we can continue our walk to Pride's city?" says Lina.

Shadow nods, seeing that his position does seem strange to a native, then lets go of Lina.

Though I'm still curious as to why he's so insistent on wearing it. How can he see so well with it on? What's he hiding under it? Ah screw it, it doesn't seem like I'll be getting it off him anytime soon. Maybe I should just ask him about it and he'll tell me. If he doesn't I guess I'll drop it for now and hope he opens up about it or I can catch him off guard and take it off him myself, thinks Lina.

They resume their walk to the city, with Lina still looking at Shadow. "So why are you dressed like that then? Are you trying to pass yourself off as a reaper or something? If so, are you trying to get work from one of the sins or with one of the four great houses?" asks Lina.

"Personal reasons. Also why do you keep saying that I look like a reaper, and what are these great houses you are talking about?" asks Shadow.

Lina is confused. "Huh, wait, don't you know about the reapers or the great houses of armageddon?!" asks Lina.

Shadow shakes his head at her. "I know what reapers are, there's mythology around them. I'm not why you'd think I'd be one though, or that they would be around here," responds Shadow.

"Oh, well here in hell reapers are probably different from what is seen or heard about in the Earth realm," says Lina.

"In what way?" asks Shadow.

"Well reapers are wildly different in appearance and personality from one another. While one could dress in bright colors and have a kind attitude another can dress all dark with a more serious attitude and vice versa. Though no matter what they are like or how they dress there's one thing that they all have in common. They keep their true faces hidden one way or another. It can range from hiding it behind their hair, a mask, or anything they have on hand, like a fan for example, but no matter what method they use their faces remain hidden. Thus why I assumed you were a reaper when I first saw your face or that you were making yourself look like one. As for the four great houses, they are the four families that have kept and expanded their influence since armageddon. There were many devils that gained titles and land after the war, but most either died off, lost their titles, or were absorbed into a more powerful family. Now only four remain and they each use a different colored horse as a symbol of their family. This gives them an interesting nickname that is heard even on Earth. You might know them as the four horsemen," explains Lina.

"Huh, well I'm not a reaper nor looking for work with any of them," responds Shadow. *That might be why Master Eve commented on my clothing choice yesterday. Though I wonder why she didn't mention the four houses. Then again she has kept to herself for a long time so maybe she doesn't know,* thinks Shadow.

"Another reason I thought you might have been one is because of the tragedies that happened in this territory some time ago. Due to those, they are seen roaming around this area from time to time collecting the dead. Thus why my initial reaction of thinking I might have died," says Lina.

"That makes sense, I have a better understanding of your reaction to me. Now that it's cleared up, let's make sure we get to the city before running into a real one," responds Shadow.

Lina just nods and the two of them continue walking in silence.

As they continue walking Shadow still hears the distant scream that he was hearing before. "Huh, why am I still hearing that?" mumbles Shadow.

"Still hearing what, Shadow?" asks Lina.

"Do you still not hear that scream in the distance?" asks Shadow.

"Oh that's probably coming from the sun. I guess you can only really hear it when it's really quiet. It would be drowned out in a town, village, or in our case a city." answers Lina.

"What do you mean it's coming from the sun?" asks Shadow.

"Well, sinners are used as the source for the sun. Usually several sinners at a time are placed into it to feed it so it can burn. They are usually left there for roughly one to two weeks. Down here their souls are indestructible so it won't kill them (as if they could die while dead). It's also part of the final steps to finishing their sentence in hell. It helps burn the roots of their sins. So they're fully rid of their sins before leaving and the citizens of hell gain a light source so it's seen as a win-win. Though I guess for someone from earth you probably see it as cruel and sadistic, but for us it's the norm," explains Lina.

"It's not my place to judge, especially if it benefits both sides in the end," responds Shadow.

"When we get into the city I'll show you to the shop to sell our loot. Then I'll take you to the butcher after that. I'm pretty sure I know where it is," says Lina.

Once we get to the city I'll have her show me where the shop is and I'll definitely ask for directions to the butcher. Then I'll immediately separate from her and leave her in the city. She'll be safer there and I'll be better off alone like usual. Plus I still have a bad feeling about that amulet so splitting up from her sooner rather than later seems like the best option. Plus talking to her has gotten me emotionally drained and we haven't even reached the city yet, thinks Shadow.

If he's going to see Pride anyways then I could probably use him. Having him around would definitely make things a lot easier. Even though he's not as much of a talker as I am, he's both nice and strong, thinks Lina. "Is that why you're heading to Pride's city first? Is it so you can deal with the new guy?" asks Lina.

"No, I... Wait, what do you mean 'new guy'?" asks Shadow.

"Oh, well he's actually the second generation of the sin of pride. To be accurate he's the only second-generation sin," explains Lina.

Just as she says that, Shadow and Lina reach the limits of Pride's city. Reaching the entrance, Shadow notices a couple of poles with some kind of ball at the top. Shadow just assumes that they are some kind of lanterns to show people the way to the city at night.

"Well here we are, Pride's city, or as it's officially called, NEW Pride City. I'll show you where the shop I told you about is in a little bit. For now I need to find a bench or something and rest for a bit," says Lina.

Shadow nods, agreeing to rest after that long walk.

Lina then pulls Shadow close to her. "Oh, also, it might be a good idea to not mention that you're from earth to anyone else," whispers Lina.

Shadow nods while pulling himself away from Lina, then the two of them officially walk into the city. Though as they do Shadow notices that there are two guards posted near the entrance. They're wearing full armor with one wielding a spear and the other an axe. Shadow starts feeling nervous, but they only nod at him and Lina and let them pass on through.

"There are some benches in the city square. It's just a short walk up ahead. Come on Shadow follow me," says Lina while pointing ahead of them.

Shadow does as she says and follows her to the city square to hopefully rest, calm down, and maybe get some questions answered.

Insight on the Two Prides

In Pride's city, officially known as New Pride City, Shadow and Lina are sitting on a bench in the city's square. They are taking a break after all the walking and fighting. Lina sits on the bench normally. Shadow on the other hand sits in a way to take up as little room as possible on the bench. Shadow looks around and is in awe and confused at what he can see around him. From what he sees the city has a variety of buildings made of stone, wood, and/or both. There are also very healthy trees with patches of grass and even a water fountain, which is the most confusing thing to Shadow. There are more of the same poles that Shadow saw at the entrance, assuring him that they are some kind of lantern to be used at night. He can even see some small vehicles like bikes, scooters, and carriages being used and moving under their own power while being directed by the resident devils. He also briefly notices that each one of them have some kind of gem attached to them, emanating an odd aura. In the distance Shadow can see a bit of a train track as well. He can even hear the train as it reaches the station that can't be seen currently.

Hard to believe a place like this exists in hell, especially compared to what I've seen so far, Shadow thinks.

Farther off, Shadow can see a purple aura possibly coming from Pride's base. It far exceeds what he's seen up to this point

Is all of that energy coming from Pride themself? If so then I'm in more trouble than originally thought. thinks Shadow.

Lastly are the devils that, just like Lina, could easily pass for humans. Shadow notices the style of clothes that they wear are similar to what is worn on earth. Some of them wear clothing styles that he's never seen in person, but ones he knows are worn in different parts of earth. Shadow also notices that every devil has faded blotches of different colors on their skin indicating their sin energy, but they're nowhere near as prominent as Lina's. If he didn't know that he was in hell Shadow would believe that he was still on earth.

"It's a lot to take in, isn't it, huh?" asks Lina.

Shadow nods as he sits there trying to figure out how this is possible.

"The sins are actually really helpful to all the devils that live in their territories. They only have a bad reputation on earth because of their job of having to place the seed of their sin into living beings there. Though down here they are seen as saviors to the devils and punishers to wrongdoers and sinners. Cities like this are able to thrive thanks to the sin in charge of that territory and their power coming from their gem outputter," explains Lina.

Shadow looks at her with his head slightly tilted, confused by what she said.

"Take a look, you can see one on the fountain, that's where the power comes from and how it keeps the city safe from dangers like the demons we fought," says Lina.

Shadow looks and at the top of the fountain is a sphere of amethyst similar to the abandoned town.

"A city this size has several, but for a town, just one would work. Well as long as the gem stays intact at least," explains Lina.

"Are they easy to break? I saw shards at the destroyed town we were in before," says Shadow.

Lina looks down with a sad look on her face. "No, they can only be destroyed by a sin or someone of equal power. Uh, at least that's what was said when they were first introduced," says Lina.

Shadow senses that there is more to what she is saying. "Do you know what happened, Lina?" asks Shadow.

"Well it has to do with the former Pride, but no one wants to talk about it," whispers Lina.

"Is it illegal to talk about it?" asks Shadow in a whispered tone.

"It's not really illegal, it's more that devils here don't want to re-member about those times," whispers Lina in a sad tone.

Shadow sees that it's something uncomfortable for her to talk about and says, "Understood."

Lina looks around and sees that everyone is giving strange looks to them, mainly at Shadow and his mask. *Geez they're all staring at us, how can Shadow stay so calm about it? Then again it's hard to tell with that mask on, but I feel like he's handling the situation well,* thinks Lina.

Shadow notices that everyone is giving him strange looks before Lina and thinks it's most likely due to his mask, but he has been brushing it off both to him being used to it and him knowing why they are looking at him.

Lina gets up and gestures to Shadow to follow her.

Oh, is she going to show me to the shop? thinks Shadow.

The two start walking and Lina starts heading to the train station where Shadow could see a bit of the tracks earlier and starts walking to an alley. In that alley there are multiple crates made of both wood and metal, which were probably about to be put on or had already been taken off the train.

Is she leading me to the shop, a butcher, or is she trying to lead me to a quiet place to jump me? thinks Shadow.

After walking a bit into the alley Shadow stops and Lina turns around to see that he stopped. "How come you stopped? Something wrong, Shadow?" asks Lina.

"Is this really the way to the shop?" asks Shadow. As he says that he positions himself so that he's prepared to run out of the alley if things go south.

"Actually I was taking you somewhere without people to tell you about the former Pride," says Lina.

"What do you know about her?" asks Shadow.

"Well first she didn't go by Pride most of the time. That was both her original name and title, but she grew bored of just being called that. She took on a name that she learned from people on earth that she felt fit her. In case you're wondering, her name was," says Lina while the train's whistle goes off, making it impossible for anyone but Shadow to hear the former Pride's name. "She was also arrogant. While in control she took on the title of Prideful Empress and had most devils in her territory refer to her as that, but those same devils that were under her control gave her the unofficial title of the Arrogant Bitch behind her back," says Lina.

"Was she that strong?" asks Shadow.

"Yes she was, well to a degree anyway," answers Lina.

"How was she strong and what made her strong?" asks Shadow, a little confused by Lina's answer.

"Well in the beginning she was one of the strongest in all of hell. She was even seen as the second strongest of the seven sins. Though as time went on she was only physically and magically stronger than the average devil and monsters. Even other sins trained and passed her in power because she saw not much reason to improve. In terms of power, by the time she fell she was probably the fifth or sixth strongest sin depending on how you measured their powers by that point. Though she acted like she was still the second strongest sin compared to the leader of the sins, who also happened to be female and treated the others as beneath her. She was especially hateful to the male sins, which she saw as low as dirt for no reason. Though in my opinion she probably just associated it with their gender. She even ignored that they had already surpassed her, only because of her belief that she was still better than them because of her gender alone. As for the source of her power, that all came from the power she had as a sin which she had when she was created after armageddon," explains Lina.

"Yeah I've heard about it already," says Shadow.

"That's a different sto... Wait, what?! Oh wait I guess Eve would have already told you about armageddon already. Well anyways please don't interrupt me so I can continue what I was telling you," answers Lina.

Shadow just gives an uncomfortable nod and Lina continues talking.

"Ok, as I said, she didn't really improve her power much from what she started off with because she believed she was still the second strongest of the sins and didn't feel she needed to improve much," answers Lina.

Shadow took a second to process what Lina just said.

"So she started out as one of the strongest sins, but eventually changed to being one of the weakest, only being stronger than a couple of sins as well as average devils and monsters. She ignored that she was now one of the weakest sins due to her lack of effort to improve. Finally, she also was only that strong due to the power she had from being a sin, but believed she was stronger than most and didn't even bother to improve out of arrogance and an unwillingness to see the truth."

"Really?" asks Shadow.

"Yeah, I know, it does sound kind of dumb when you say it out loud. Though back when she was still in charge that much power was kind of enough, at least until her end anyways," says Lina.

Shadow re-centers himself after what he just heard and looks right at Lina. "What do you know about the new Pride and how did he become the only second-generation sin?" asks Shadow.

Lina looks away slightly. "Well before I tell you that, I will first want to tell you what led up to that situation and why no one wants to talk about it," says Lina. "Some time ago this territory was ruled over by the original sin of pride and was seen as a nightmare by most. While at a meeting with the other sins, they were discussing the situation on Pride's territory. Pride ruled over the people in this territory horribly with her strength and power as a sin, though it was mainly toward the men. She treated them like lesser beings, which was thanks to her perception of males being weaker than her and being hopeless without her. She had no real reason to but she would treat them like dirt, which was something that the sins shouldn't do to those living in their territory. It was especially terrible for those that lived in this city. Devils in other towns of this territory were even terrified of whenever she would make an appearance in their towns. An example is that whenever she went out to one of the towns or villages in this territory most men would lock themselves into the buildings there. If they didn't she would hurt them for little to no reason. If she was also in a bad mood she would destroy the gem that was used to keep the town or village safe from dangers. She destroyed them with her personal sin weapon, which was a small sword that also doubled as a whip that she would wear like a belt when not in use. Unfortunately the common devils couldn't do anything because of her position as both a sin and the ruler of the territory. If she destroyed their gem they had four choices: either move into the city and under her thumb, move to a different town or village and hope nothing happened to that one, try to move to a new territory and start a new life, or stay out there and end up dying," continues Lina.

"Things got even worse when a small group of around ten to fifteen other women became her direct followers and took advantage of her position. To prove they were her followers they wore purple sleeveless jackets with a crown on the back as a symbol of superiority over other devils in Pride's territory. They made things worse so that most men wouldn't even leave their homes and/or business, but that didn't help when Pride's followers got involved. If there was some male that they didn't like they would make up a lie to their leader that would make them seem like the victim. Even if it was obvious that it was a lie, Pride would still believe her woman and punish the male that didn't do anything. Due to her followers' manipulation and lies, Pride destroyed more and more of her territory's towns and her villages' gems. Eventually the only place in this territory that was still safe was this city. Though many weren't thrilled to have to live within the city due to how they were being treated. It became so bad that all the males left the city altogether instead of dealing with the harassment and settled into that town where we met. Those that left begged for a gem to keep them safe so they could willingly leave the city. After watching them grovel at her feet Pride allowed it and gave them the gem with a very smug look on her face, though the gem she gave them was a weaker one so it wasn't as effective as ones she'd destroyed before. The town in ruins where we met was actually where those that left settled so they could still be close to their family still in the city.

"At first Pride and her followers saw it as a win, but it wasn't long before they all saw the ramifications of them all leaving. Soon she noticed that a lot of the hard labor jobs were left with few to no devils to do them. With few or no devils doing those jobs the city was slowly becoming worse by the day. She soon ordered the females that were left, including her group of followers, to do them, but there still weren't enough devils to do them and some didn't want to do them because they said it was too hard. Both her territory and city were becoming shells of what they used to be, if they weren't already.

"As things got worse the first thing she did was whine to the other sins during one of their meetings, hoping they would fix the problem for her. When the male sins called her out on her behavior and treatment of those that had left the city due to her actions, even those that went to their territories after putting them in danger, and the many that died for the same reason, Pride only ignored their accusations. She instead tried to turn it around to make herself seem like the victim and not them for not respecting her as a sin. Though none of the other sins believed her because she'd done that many times already. That just made her whine about her problem even more. Finally the leader of the sins, Sloth, who was one of the other female sins, roughly placed her hand on Pride's head and turned it toward her and told her she had to fix this problem herself. Since she'd caused this problem she must rectify it. If she refused and/or continued with this issue, she would either be stripped of her territory and authority or she would be replaced as a sin entirely. Pride thought she was bluffing, but Sloth wasn't. She already had plans in place, knowing she would probably do the bare minimum to stay out of trouble, if not do anything at all, thinking that someone else should do it for her.

"While Pride was away at her meeting with the other sins her followers were basically left running the city themselves, which wasn't unheard of for a sin to leave someone in charge while they were away, but they abused their authority mercilessly. They forced the women still living in the city that weren't part of their group to work more and wait on them hand and foot. They treated them no better than slaves. It was so bad that those oppressed women ran away from the city at night while the followers were asleep just like the men prior. They tried to go to the town the men had created for shelter, but because the men were terrified that it might have been Pride and her followers, they locked up every building and waited, hoping they would leave out of fear. The men there saw that it wasn't Pride or her followers and slowly opened up everything to them, but knew that if they left then Pride most likely wouldn't be far behind to take them back, most likely leaving that town in ruins to leave them no choice. With nowhere else to turn to, the closest place they could go was to Lust's territory to take shelter and find help there.

"When Pride returned she saw that her city was mostly abandoned except for her handful of followers. Predictably she was enraged by this and questioned her followers why only they were left. Her followers, worried of telling her the real reason, lied to her and said they were kidnapped by the men that left the city prior. Believing them, she went straight to the town of men, thinking the men had kidnapped them instead of them abandoning the city after being treated horribly by her and her followers. When she got to their town she saw that it was completely abandoned. More enraged, she destroyed the gem that they'd begged for to keep their town safe with her bare hands. After destroying the gem she then saw tracks with the direction leading to Lust's territory. She headed back to her base to grab her weapon and ordered her followers to follow her. She then headed for Lust's territory, following the tracks with her followers not far behind. She followed the tracks while riding in her own personal vehicle being driven by one of her followers. The vehicle was an obnoxious shade of purple, in my opinion, and was modeled after what is called on earth a limo. It was large enough to hold her as well as her followers. The tracks led straight to Lust's main city, which had enraged her even more, thinking that Lust was now directly involved.

"She burst into the city demanding that Lust come out to return her property. The people that came from her territory were terrified and started running while her followers started harassing anyone that got near them and were about to just start tying people up to take back, whether they were originally from Pride's territory or not. Finally Lust came out to deal with the commotion, but it wasn't just them, it was all of the other sins. Pride was confused why they were all here, especially with their meeting being finished not too long ago. Sloth then told her that they'd had enough of her actions and told her and her followers to stand down. Obviously they didn't and Pride once again tried to make herself seem like the victim because her citizens had abandoned her. The people that came from her territory saw this as a chance to expose Pride for her wrongdoings. They called her out on both her and her followers' terrible treatment of all of them. Pissed at what they were saying, she started hitting those that bad-mouthed her, with her followers doing the same. All the while the other sins were able to see it all. Having seen enough of this, Sloth brought out a thin man who was probably just slightly taller than you, Shadow, and told Pride to fight him.

"When she asked why, Sloth just told her that he was her replacement and that if she couldn't beat him she would be stripped of both her title and power. She just laughed at the person, believing that he would never win. She probably believed that because she thought he was weaker than her due to her being a sin and her opponent being a man. She got right up next to him and started looking down at him for both being a man and even thinking of taking a sin's place. Immediately after her boasting, Pride got sent flying from a single punch from her opponent. Everyone was confused, then suddenly Pride started running at him with her weapon in hand. Her replacement also went charging at her and they started fighting each other. Their fight lasted a while, with both sides trading blows and her opponent going down after some time. When it seemed that he was defeated and exhausted from the fight she started boasting to everyone that she was unbeatable. Though while she was boasting, her opponent rose back up while laughing, telling her that she couldn't beat him if that was her best. Pride looked over and saw him with a dumbfounded look on her face. He just stood there, completely fine, as if the fight hadn't started yet. He even looked at her with a smug look on his face to mock her, basically saying she couldn't win against him. Pride was enraged that he'd gotten back up and charged back at him again, but this time it was more one-sided. She couldn't even hit him at this point while he was landing hit after hit. She started to believe that she would lose and be stripped of her title. So as a last-ditch effort she dropped her amulet on the ground and tried to destroy it. For her it was her way of saying, 'If I can't be Pride, then no one will be ever again.' Unfortunately for her though, her opponent delivered one last blow to her before she could even hit it. With that last strike she finally collapsed, losing the fight.

"With the battle over, Sloth walked over to her and took both Pride's amulet that signified her title of a sin and her sin weapon, then gave them to her opponent. Then the other five sins gathered around her created a magic circle with a pentagram inside of it around the now former Pride, with the leading sin forming one around the new Pride. The former Pride tried to crawl away but to no avail. She couldn't leave while the circle was up. Then a light that came from both circles ended up draining all of the former Pride's power and giving it to the now new Pride, officially making him both the new sin of pride as well as the first second-generation sin. The transfer over the circle disappeared and the other sins went over to the new Pride to congratulate him on his victory and new status.

"The former Pride, now in a far weaker state, looked at her followers and told them to help her up and take her back to her base. Her followers were hesitant until one of them told her not to tell them what to do. Former Pride, in shock at what was said, realized that the devils that followed her were only doing it to use the authority she had as a sin and without that, they wanted nothing to do with her. Realizing that, she started to cry and the top of her head started glowing and something seemed to start sprouting from there. Her followers went right to the new Pride and started sucking up to him to try to get on his good side to use him like the former Pride. He didn't want anything to do with them and had them arrested to pay for the crimes they'd committed under the former Pride's authority. I hear that they are currently working at Greed's casino to make up for their wrongdoings. While the followers were arrested, Sloth and Wrath took the former Pride and took her away somewhere. With that, the territory is now controlled by the new Pride. It's still a long way from its former glory, but the new Pride has been making an effort since that day to build this territory back up," explains Lina, taking some deep breaths after her monologue.

"Ok, now that I'm finished with that, any questions?" asks Lina.

"How do you know so much about all that?" asks Shadow.

"I meant about the new Pride, but to answer that, uhhh, well, it's the first time a sin was replaced so everyone in hell knows this story," answers Lina awkwardly.

"What about the parts where only sins were there?" asks Shadow.

"Uhhhhh, well, the sin of Envy from where I'm from is a bit of a gossip and let it slip. There's even a book written by the sin of Lust detailing it," answers Lina more awkwardly.

"Oh ok," says Shadow. *She's clearly hiding something, but why? Wait, what if the answer is something I shouldn't know?* thinks Shadow, somewhat worried. "Whatever happened to the former Pride?" asks Shadow.

"I'm not entirely sure, but from what I heard she either somehow got away from them and is living somewhere in shame, she could have been left for dead to fight off demons without her powers, or she is being held captive by one of the sins to pay for her crimes," explains Lina.

Geez, none of those outcomes sound good. I mean, after what she did she probably had it coming, but still, thinks Shadow. "Ok, last question I have about her. Why did she try to destroy the amulet? Would it have meant that no one could be Pride?" asks Shadow.

"Well as far as I know it's the only way to transfer the powers, but destroying it would spell disaster for the sin themself and/or everyone around them. Though I'm not sure about the latter because until then no sin even tried to destroy it," explains Lina.

Shadow just stands there contemplating how desperate the former sin must have been to attempt something so dangerous.

"Ok, do you have any questions about the new Pride?" asks Lina.

"What is his name, how strong is he, what powers does he have, and does he have any weaknesses?" asks Shadow.

"Wow, so many questions at once. Uh, ok, going in order. Firstly his name is Yuki. When it comes to his strength, that's hard to say. I heard he's much stronger than when he first became Pride, as shown by his base, which changed from a pawn to a rook some time ago, but he isn't as strong as Sloth. I'm also uncertain of where he stands against the other sins so I can't give you an accurate answer, but either way he is very powerful. As for his powers, I know for sure that he has that skill I mentioned in the story, which he developed from training prior to being a sin. It allows him to basically revive and heal to perfect health if he doesn't get killed before activating it. Which, like I mentioned earlier, was what he used in his fight with the former Pride to beat her. That power is the origin of his title 'The Dangerous Zombie,' which is very fitting in my opinion. Other than that I heard that he developed new skills and abilities, though not much is known about it. All I heard is that it is some form of telepathy and that's all I know. As for his weaknesses, well that's easy, because he worked hard to obtain that power and became the sin of pride. So he has developed a high opinion of himself. Though he takes great care of this territory, he sees himself and the other sins as gods. So taking advantage of that would be your best bet at winning against him," explains Lina.

Shadow sighs after hearing all of that. *Geez, he seems really over-powered. No wonder Master Eve told me to not start off with him even though he's the closest sin. Though something about that weakness sounds kinda familiar, but that doesn't make it seem any less stupid,* thinks Shadow.

Lina could somewhat tell that Shadow was worrying about it. "So shall we head to the shop and butcher?" asks Lina.

"Yeah, let's get going, I need to find a sword and new shoes," answers Shadow.

Lina looks down at Shadow's shoes and they show signs of being burnt and a bit melted.

I'll grab some equipment, then come back here to see if the train can take me to the next territory. After I take on those other two sins, then I'll come back later to face him. Maybe by then I'll be strong enough to fight him, thinks Shadow.

"Alright, let's go then. We'll head to the shop first," says Lina, going behind Shadow and pushing on his back to head to the shop.

Shadow freaks out and quickly circles around Lina and gets a pitchfork ready behind his back. "Go on, lead the way," says Shadow in a slightly angry tone.

"Oh ok," says Lina, slightly confused by Shadow's reaction.

Maybe he doesn't like people behind him or doesn't like his back being touched. I should remember that for later, thinks Lina. Lina starts walking toward the shop with Shadow following right behind her after putting the pitchfork away.

Exploring the City

Lina finally leads Shadow to the city's best and only shop for equipment. Just as the two of them get to the door, a devil wearing light brown, somewhat loose-fitting clothes walks out. Shadow believes he recognizes the devils clothing as a thawb. They were also carrying a halberd on their back. Given the weapon's condition the devil most likely just bought it. At first it's unclear if it's a man or woman since they also have their face covered as well. Without saying a word the devil walks towards them and walks past the two of them. As they walked past, Shadow saw their aura and saw that it was somewhat different from the other devils in the city. He also feels like this devil is familiar from somewhere, but can't figure out where. Deciding to ignore all of that for now, the two of them walk into the store.

"Wel... come," says Nite while looking at Shadow. At first he's caught off guard by Shadow's mask, but shakes it off. The shop is larger than it first appeared outside; it has bookshelves, racks, and barrels full of items like clothes, camping and cooking equipment, similar-looking gems that he saw before except not giving off any aura from them, a variety of weapons, scrolls and books, merchandise of the sins (mainly the new Pride), and other miscellaneous items for sale. Nite is standing behind a counter near the back of the store. From what Shadow can see of him he looks rather muscular, with multiple scars across his body. He has a buzz cut and wears a dark purple sleeveless shirt. He stares at the two of them since they're the only customers in his shop.

"So what do you need to get?" asks Lina.

Shadow looks around and sees pairs of fireproof boots. He walks over to them and picks up a pair of black boots that are his shoe size. "I'll take these, and do you buy stuff from people, sir?" asks Shadow.

"The name's Nite, and sure, but what do you have?" asks Nite.

"I have quite a few pitchforks from some imps that I killed before coming into town," says Shadow.

"Ok then, where are they?" asks Nite.

Shadow proceeds to start piling the pitchforks from the normal imps on the counter, keeping the one from the imp leader and the fang piece from the orthrus leader hidden, just in case.

Nite is surprised to see Shadow's storage seal. "Hey, a storage seal, that's not something you see every day," says Nite.

Shadow just keeps pulling out the pitchforks till all of the red imps' pitchforks are on the counter.

Nite is taken aback slightly by just the sheer number of pitchforks and how Shadow brought them out. "Did you get all of these at once?" asks Nite.

Shadow nods his head, waiting to see what he can get for them.

"My, that's impressive. Back in my younger days it would have taken me a week to get this many. With this you can get these boots and still have plenty left over," says Nite in a slightly sad tone. Shadow notices the slight sadness and can tell through his aura that hearing how Shadow killed so many alone and in such a short amount of time hurt Nite's pride a bit.

I probably shouldn't have said that they were taken all down at once. It's clear that's not the norm here and I don't want to stand out any more than I already do, thinks Shadow. "I meant that I collected all the pitchforks all at once, but it took me some time to kill off all the imps. I'm not sure how long I was out there, but I do know that it was days," says Shadow.

Nite perks up from what Shadow said. "Oh that makes more sense, I misunderstood. Hahaha, as if someone could kill this many imps in one day," exclaims Nite, bursting with pride.

All the while Lina just stood away from them looking dumbfounded as to why Shadow had bothered lying.

"Ok now if you could just give me your hunter card I will update it for you," says Nite.

Hunter card, what's that, thinks Shadow. "Um, I don't have one, I'm sorry," says Shadow, getting nervous.

"Huh, why don't you have one?" asks Nite, starting to get suspicious.

"It got destroyed after he finished collecting the pitchforks. When he finished he took it out to start calculating if they would be enough to raise his rank. Then an imp that was hiding came out and tried to strike Shadow. Though it missed him it did hit his card and then ran away out of fear," says Lina out of nowhere.

The two of them look over to her and Nite relaxes. "Oh, is that all that happened? Why didn't you say something? I thought you were a thief or scam artist for a second there," says Nite.

Shadow looks back at Nite. "Sorry, it's just uh embarrassing to admit that it happened." responds Shadow.

"Oh it's nothing to be embarrassed about. Stuff like that happens from time to time. We can just make you a new one here. Just hold on while I get the thing set up," says Nite.

Nite pulls out a large stone and metal slab and places it onto the counter. The slab is large enough for Shadow to place his hand on with a slot at the end towards Nite. He then pulls out a sheet of what looks to be metal that's the size and shape of a trading card. Shadow figures that it's a blank hunter card. Nite places it into the slot and the slab begins to glow around the edges. "Ok it's ready now please just place your hand onto the slab," says Nite.

Shadow does so and places his right hand onto the slab. As soon as he touches the slab the light vanishes. This worries Shadow thinking he did something wrong or that he'll be outed as a human. Suddenly darkness starts emanating from the slab. Words from both hell and earth start appearing in both red and white. The darkness grows larger and larger, almost reaching the ceiling. All three of them are confused at what's going on and as soon as it had started the darkness goes back into the slab and the card begins to shine.

"Uh, well your card is done I guess," says Nite, still confused by what just happened.

Nite takes the card out of the slot and hands it to Shadow. The card is still blank which worries Shadow.

"Oh, don't worry too much about it being blank. I rarely get to make them so I don't bother getting newer slates if this one still works just fine. The drawback of using an older one is that it'll take a few hours till the info appears. Sorry for the inconvenience," says Nite.

"Ah, no it's fine. Thank you for making me a new card," responds Shadow.

"So did that happen last time you had a card made. I know that it was my first time seeing something like that while creating a hunter card," says Nite.

Seriously, Just what in hell was all of that Shadow, thinks Lina.

"No, that's never happened before. I'm not sure what that was about. I'm sorry if it caused any issues," says Shadow, feeling nervous and a little guilty.

"Ah well, don't worry so much about it. So anyways will that be all then?" asks Nite.

"Actually I have a question about something else that I found and want to know if it has any value in it," asks Shadow.

"Sure, I'm pretty knowledgeable on most equipment and materials for them. So what's the item in question?" responds Nite.

Shadow proceeds to pull out and place the orthrus fang onto the counter. Nite falls over in surprise. Lina, though less surprised, backs to the wall so as to not fall over. Shadow quickly realizes that he made a mistake. He grabs the fang and puts it back into his cloak. Nite gets back up and looks Shadow right in the eyes, or as best as he can.

"You just found that?" asks Nite, sounding nervous.

"Yes, it was on the ground while I passed through a fog that showed me illusions," responds Shadow, not wanting to tell the truth how he got it.

Without either of them looking Lina stiffens up slightly. She turns her head away to keep it hidden that she's nervous. With Nite starting to regain his composure, though, he starts to become confused by what Shadow said.

"Hmm that's strange, fogs really are rare in this territory. I also never heard of one that shows illusions. Though I think I might have heard a rumor of something like that a while back," says Nite.

With her face still hidden Lina starts nervously sweating a little.

"Well I'm not much for rumors. Can I sell this fang here?" asks Shadow.

Nite shakes his head to the question. "Sorry, but I don't have the money to pay for something like that. Even if I tried, my wife would have my head on a pike. My suggestion is that you find a blacksmith. Orthrus fangs are good materials for armor or weapons. Though you won't find any in this city that would be willing to try. I'd probably try looking for one in Wrath's territory. That's where most of the best blacksmiths live. Though until then how's about you buy one here to get you by," says Nite.

"Thank you for both your honesty and your advice, and I'll take you up on your offer to buy a weapon. Though do you happen to also have any swords for sale? When I walked in and looked around I noticed none around," says Shadow.

"I do, but I only have two left right now so you don't have much choice. A small group of warrior level hunters came by earlier and bought most of my stock. They bought around three to four times as many weapons as they had members, then tried to force me to give them a discount, claiming that their leader was trained by the legendary Eve herself. Though personally I didn't care and told them to pay and leave. Unfortunately because of them the ones I currently have aren't my best products until I get more made or delivered. So I just didn't see much reason to put them out," says Nite.

Ugh, so there are some of them here in this city. I hope we don't run into them, thinks Lina with disgust.

"That's fine, could I see them please?" asks Shadow.

Nite moves away from the counter to go get the swords. Nite pulls out the two swords: a broadsword made of gold with a silver hilt and decorative sheath, and an arming sword made of iron with an iron hilt of plain metal and a leather-like bound sheath. "This is all I've got so do you want either of them?" asks Nite.

Shadow looks over both swords and Lina looks over with a worried look. *Wait, he's not going to choose that one is he? I should say or do something to stop him,* thinks Lina. While thinking of what to say she starts moving to push some fragile items over without thinking about it, probably in an attempt to make him pay for the damages.

"I'll take the arming sword, please and thank you," says Shadow.

Lina hears that and stops what she's doing.

Nite puts the gold sword away and gives him the iron arming sword. "With that and the heat-resistant boots, normally you would be charged twenty copper. Though since you brought so many pitch-forks to sell, I'll take it out of what I would've paid for them and give you the rest," says Nite, calculating Shadow's change. Nite then hands Shadow a small stack of coins with one square gray-colored one and ten circular copper-colored ones.

Is... Is that a lot? Were those pitchforks really worth that much? I don't know the worth of the currency here. Could it be he knows that I don't know and is paying me less? He might and he might think he can rip me off. No, that's stupid, why would I think that if I don't know what things here are worth? Though what if I'm right and he's taking advantage of my lack of knowledge? Crap, I'm taking too long, I should just take it for now, thinks Shadow.

As Shadow gets his change he notices that the currency here has a different gem in the middle than what Eve gave him. *Hmm, maybe the gem is different depending on which territory it originated in,* thinks Shadow.

"Also, to make up for that lesser-quality sword and for all the pitch-forks you sold me, take this skill scroll and this used movement gem as free gifts," says Nite as he also hands Shadow a gem from behind the counter.

Shadow just looks at it, just wondering both what it is and what he's supposed to do with it. All he can tell is that it's brown and has some faded marking on the inside of it. Nite notices this and starts feeling uncomfortable, thinking that Shadow is unhappy with his free gift.

"Hey, sorry that it's used, but I can't just give you a new movement gem for free," says Nite.

"No it's not, that it's just that, I don't really know what this is for, sorry," apologizes Shadow.

"Huh, oh you must be from a real closed off and rural town or village aren't you," says Nite nonchalantly.

"Er yeah, I'm from really far away and never really saw or used one of these before. If it's not too much trouble could you explain what this is and what I can do with it?" asks Shadow.

"Not at all! Basically this gem was a combined creation of three of the sins. Sloth, Lust, and Gluttony worked hard to make these wonders. They are able to move small or large vehicles by absorbing energy from the devil controlling it. All you need to do is secure it onto the vehicle and make a connection to it with your energy and you're all set. The amount needed varies on how big the vehicle is and how much is needed to create momentum. I'm sure you've seen them around the city by now," says Nite.

After explaining this Nite thinks something is odd about this.

"Hey, wait, if you didn't know about these until now then how did you get here? Did you come here on the train without knowing what powered it or something?" asks Nite.

Shadow shakes his head and looks at Nite.

"No, I walked all the way here," says Shadow.

Nite and to a lesser extent Lina are surprised to hear that he walked all the way to the city. Lina knows the real reason why he wouldn't know anything about moment gems or what they're used for, but she's still a bit surprised that he walked as long as he did with what he had. Nite however is just left dumbfounded, but has a gut feeling that Shadow wasn't lying or messing with him. Suddenly he just starts laughing.

"HAHAHA, to think there are still some devils out there that have the balls to willingly travel great distances of hell on foot alone. You know what, I like you kid, here, take this skill scroll from me as another free gift from me as a sign of recognizing your bravery and strength," says Nite, handing Shadow a scroll.

"Thank you for all of this. Oh, I do have one more question. Do you know where a good butcher is? I have something to sell there too," says Shadow, taking his boots, sword, gem, and scroll.

"Sure, I know someone, they're also in my opinion the best one in the city. Just walk south from here for around three minutes and you should see it on your left," answers Nite.

Shadow thanks Nite and walks out of the shop with Lina following right behind him, but she gets called out by Nite. "So are you planning to sell your pitchforks or do you plan on just loitering and trying to break my merch?" asks Nite.

Lina, surprised, quickly walks up to the counter. "Yeah sorry, I kind of got distracted and I wasn't intending to break anything," answers Lina.

He just looks at her and sarcastically says, "MM HMM."

Guess I got busted haha, thinks Lina nervously as she sells her pitchforks.

Outside the shop Shadow switches his shoes. Lina walks out of the shop and looks at Shadow with an irritated look. After lacing up his new boots Shadow starts heading in the direction Nite told him to head in.

Lina walks right up to him, still bearing an irritated look. "WHY did you ask him for directions? I KNEW where to go already!" exclaims Lina.

"I wanted a second opinion from a local so I wouldn't have to waste more of your time," responds Shadow.

Lina calms down and looks back at Shadow. "It's fine, you saved me from those imps so I'm just repaying the favor. So let's just head to the butcher and sell off the rest of the loot."

Shadow nods and the two of them continue to walk to the butcher. Lina then turns her head back to Shadow.

"So why did you choose that sword instead of the other?" asks Lina, pointing at Shadow's new sword.

"Gold isn't as strong and has a lower melting point than iron, which would make that sword less useful for what I need," explains Shadow.

"Oh, that makes some sense I guess, but isn't iron's melting point only somewhat higher than gold and susceptible to rust if not taken care of? I mean it's one of the most replaced metal weapons down here. Even though it was cheaper I'm not sure it was worth it in the long run. That's also not taking into account the fact that it's of lesser quality than it should be," says Lina.

"It's good enough for what I need right now," responds Shadow.

"Fair enough, but he also handed you that skill scroll too," says Lina.

"What's a skill scroll anyways?" asks Shadow.

"It gives you a skill, kind of like a game. They are powered by the abundance of powerful aura all throughout hell. Just open the scroll, focus on and say the text of the skill, and you will instantly learn it. So what skill did he give you?" asks Lina.

"I'll check it later," responds Shadow.

"Ah BOO, let's check it now," says Lina, reaching over to Shadow's cloak. She lifts his cloak and sees nothing there. "Ah, right, this cloak has a storage spell. Guess I have no choice but to wait till you pull it out," says Lina, slightly disappointed as the two of them continue to walk.

Soon enough the two of them arrive at the butcher. The butcher's shop is separated into two buildings. The first is a smaller building around the same size as the shop from before for purchases of meats and whatnot. The other is a much larger warehouse-like building.

That must be where they butcher the larger demons. I'll definitely need that if I plan to sell to them, thinks Shadow.

The scent of blood is strongly emanating from the building.

"Geez, how could we not smell this from the shop?" asks Lina, holding her nose.

Shadow, ignoring the smell, walks right into the business entrance.

"HEY, wait up," says Lina, following Shadow in.

When they walk in they quickly notice how much cooler it is here compared to outside. There doesn't seem to be anyone else in here with them, not even an employee. Shadow takes his time and looks around and sees different cuts of meat as well as some household equipment and seasonings and spices also for sale. Farther in there is a counter with a bell that can summon the butcher or one of their possible employees. Shadow goes up to the counter and rings the bell. The bell rings so loud the two of them think the ground is shaking. Both of them place their hands on their ears from the noise. It was far louder than either of them expected.

"Coming," says a feminine-sounding voice from the other room.

The door to the warehouse opens and out walks the butcher. She is a somewhat muscular-looking woman that seems just a little shorter than Shadow. She wears a long shirt, a pair of plain pants, a white apron, a hairnet, and cloth gloves. Everything that she wears is white, but is stained with blotches of purple to varying degrees, all except her gloves, which are dyed a deep magenta.

"How can I help you today?" asks the butcher.

"We're here to sell some demons we killed," responds Shadow, not missing a beat.

"So where are they? Are they outside or something?" asks the butcher.

"No, I have them in my storage since there's a lot of them," answers Shadow.

She only nods and walks back to the door she just came through. She turns back to them and gestures to them to come to her. "Follow me, you can show me what you got in the warehouse. Oh, and call me Tanza, it'll make things go faster," says Tanza.

Shadow and Lina nod and follow Tanza. All three of them walk into the warehouse of the butcher shop.

Immediately the smell of blood intensifies. The warehouse is shown to contain several different demons, all in different degrees of butchering. Tanza walks by a large table and looks over at Shadow.

"So show me what you've got to sell," says Tanza.

Shadow nods and walks over to the table. He proceeds to pull out ALL of the imps that he killed.

Tanza is taken aback in surprise by the amount. "Wow, was it only the two of you that killed all of these?" asks Tanza.

Shadow only nods in response to her question.

"Impressive, and since they all still seem so fresh you must have killed them all recently too," insists Tanza.

"It took some time so I'm not sure how long it was. Whatever I killed I put into my cloak's storage. It probably took us days to a week to get them all," says Shadow so as not to look suspicious.

Tanza looks at them and can tell that Shadow is lying about how long it took, but not that he killed them. "Are you trying to lie so I won't be surprised or suspicious? Well it won't work. Storage seals are rare, but I know that time doesn't just stop in them. I can tell that these were all killed recently, like a few hours at most, not a few days. I mean, if you just had their pitchforks that lie would work, but you can't fool a trained butcher. Even my husband that runs the shop just down the street could tell. You probably went to him first and thought of the lie on the spot to not hurt his pride as a former warrior level hunter. Though after seeing how many fresh imps you dropped off, when he comes home he'll put two and two together," says Tanza.

So lying was just a waste of time then. He's going to find out anyway. It'll just upset him more finding out I lied to him to his face about it, thinks Shadow, lowering his head.

So he recommended her because she was his wife. Though she does seem to know her stuff, but it's hard to tell if his claim of her being the best in the city was true or just him being biased, thinks Lina.

Tanza sees Shadow lowering his head and can tell he probably feels bad about the situation.

"Sure, it'd hurt his self-esteem a bit, but he'll get over it… eventually," says Tanza, trying to make Shadow feel better.

Shadow takes a deep breath and nods his head. Lina just stands by while this happens, begins to feel cold from standing there for so long, and looks right at Tanza. "So now that everything is taken care of, can we please sell these imps to you now?" says Lina.

Tanza snaps back out of it and agrees.

The three of them finish the transaction, with Tanza agreeing to dismember one of the demons and place it into a cold box, which she throws in while subtracting some of the cost from the final payout. She explains that if they carry the cold box around then they can use it to store ingredients that they plan to cook when they are outside of the city without it going bad. The box looks to be made of some kind of crystal. It has writing around the opening and on the inside. It's both to help increase the size and keep it cold inside. After showing them what it can do, Tanza finishes disassembling one of the imps, then wraps it up and puts it in the cooler.

The three of them then head back to the shop side of the shop. Tanza quickly removes her blood-soaked gloves and heads to her side of the counter. "Ok, with that finished let me calculate your total so I don't have to keep you here any longer. Deducting the cost of the cooler and the imp meat, this will be your payout," says Tanza, putting around forty copper coins in a bag onto the counter.

Wow, forty copper, even after selling him that cooler. It's clear she pushed one of her more expensive ones, but still, that's still not a bad payout. Are they still in need of meat over here? I guess things aren't as fixed yet as I thought. Wait, where did Shadow go? thinks Lina.

Crap, I still don't know anything about the currency here. Is the payout I got a lot? Also, this cooler, will it work like she said, or is she just pawning some junk onto me and overcharging me for it? Fuck, I'm taking too long again. I'll just take the money and check it out later or something, thinks Shadow.

Shadow then takes the coins, puts them into his coin bag, asks her a question, thanks Tanza for her help and services, and leaves Tanza's shop while Lina is deep in thought.

Lina runs out the door, trying to catch up to Shadow. "HEY, stop leaving me behind!" yells Lina.

"I thought you only wanted to only stay together till you showed me where the shop and butchers are," responds Shadow.

"You could at least say bye then. It's rude to just ditch someone without saying goodbye," says Lina.

Shadow looks down and apologizes.

"Well for the time being we should find an inn since it's starting to get late," says Lina, pointing at the sun setting past the buildings.

"I asked Tanza where a good one is. I'm heading there now," responds Shadow.

"Alright then, let's go there now," says Lina.

After finding the inn that Shadow was told about to stay for the night, the two of them enter. The inside of the inn has stone floors and wooden walls with decorations strewn about. There is a decently sized stone and wooden counter near the door where they can rent rooms from. There is a staircase leading to a second floor where the rooms for rent are. The rest of the area that they can see is a dining area where those staying or stopping by can sit down and eat at. The two of them head to the counter and each book themselves a room. The devil at the counter gives them each a room key after they pay the fee of six copper coins for one night. With their rooms taken care of they then sit at one of their tables to grab something to eat and to discuss what they're going to do. Not long after sitting down Lina starts ordering a crazy amount of food, supposedly for herself. After a while of sitting at their table waiting for her food Lina notices that Shadow didn't order anything.

"You aren't going to eat anything?" asks Lina as her food gets delivered and fills nearly the entire table.

"Later," responds Shadow as Lina eats her food.

"Well you can't have any of mine," says Lina while stuffing her face.

Shadow nods while wondering how she can eat all of that without any shame. While Lina eats Shadow looks around the room just to know who to be wary of. While looking around he notices the person he and Lina saw outside the shop earlier. The devil is sitting at a table in the corner with only a drink sitting on the table. The only other devils there at the time are a group of four devils. Lina sees Shadow looking at them and sees them herself, but then just goes back to eating, seeing them as unimportant. Their group consists of a swordsman who seems to be the leader, with short black hair and wearing mostly greenish armor, a female archer with long red hair and wearing blue clothing/armor hanging on his left arm, a male shield-bearing tank with medium blond hair and wearing reddish armor hanging on his right, and lastly, behind all of them, being obscured, seems to be a devil wearing a slave mask, an oversized cloak making it hard to tell if it's a man or woman with them carrying a pack that appears to be used to carry the entire party's belongings. The group also has far more weapons than they have members. Their armor and clothes also seem to be high quality. This reminds Shadow of what Nite told him.

That might be the group that Nite told me about. I better stay away from them for now. I'd rather not have something start with them, thinks Shadow.

"So what's your plan for Pride?" whispers Lina.

Shadow quickly snaps out of his thoughts and looks back at Lina. "I'll come back later after going for Lust and Envy first," whispers Shadow.

Lina is so surprised by what Shadow said that she almost chokes on her food. "Wait, you're not going to do anything while you're here?" Lina barely whispers.

"No, at daybreak I'm leaving for the next sin's territory," whispers Shadow. *Though maybe I'll check out the base here to see what I could be up against. Hopefully I won't be in over my head,* thinks Shadow.

Lina sighs and gives a disappointed look to Shadow while she finishes her food. Shadow gets up from the table and walks up the stairs to his room. On his way up to his room he can hear someone yelling something about food, but chooses to ignore it since it wasn't directed at him.

After going to his room Shadow locks the door behind him. Afterward he then picks up the first heavy thing he can find and blocks the door with it almost out of habit. Looking around the room Shadow sees that his room has wooden floors, a soft-looking bed in the corner, a wooden table and chair near the opposite corner with a window covered by a curtain next to it, a nightstand next to the bed, and a dresser, which Shadow puts in front of the door. Shadow walks to the table and pulls out the food that Eve gave him before he left and sits down. What is inside is a variety of sandwiches. Shadow lifts his mask to just above his eyes and starts eating the sandwiches. While eating, Shadow also pulls out the sack of coins to count them and find Eve's cheat sheet. He counts what he got from Eve with what he collected after coming into the town and after what he paid for. He has one gray square coin and ninety-four copper circle coins. After removing all the coins, all that remains in the bag is the egg that Eve gave him, which is fine after being in the bag with all those coins and what looks like a small folded-up piece of paper. Shadow pulls the egg out first to see if it is ok and notices something different about it. When Eve gave it to him the egg was roughly the size of a chicken egg but now it's about the size of a duck egg. There are also some strange lines that have appeared on it, forming some kind of pattern.

Huh, did it get slightly bigger? Also, were these weird lines on it this morning? Is it getting close to hatching, or did I do something wrong and damage it because I left it in the bag with all those coins without thinking about it? I hope not, this was a gift from Master Eve. Well for now I'll leave it out of the bag and just keep a closer eye on it, thinks Shadow.

After placing the egg to the side carefully, Shadow pulls out the sheet left in the bag. It feels exactly like paper, but Shadow isn't sure about that after seeing the results of plant life on the way here, contrasting with what he's seen in the city.

Shadow chooses to not think about it too much and unfolds the sheet. What is written down is exactly what his Master told him: a cheat sheet about the currency in hell. Broken down, copper coins have a circle shape and have the lowest value, and indium coins have a square shape and are worth one hundred copper coins. Platinum coins have a hexagonal shape and are worth one hundred Indium coins. Lastly the rarest coins are made of rhodium and have an octagonal shape and are worth one hundred platinum coins. Each coin has a gem in it to both help keep them from melting and to keep them from being counterfeited. The type of gem just signifies where the coin was made. Also, holy metals like gold and silver are banned and any seen are either illegal or fake.

Shadow folds the sheet back up and puts it back into the bag along with all his coins. Shadow then pulls out one of his shirts that he had in his cloak and wraps the egg into it to help keep it safe, then carefully places it back into his cloak. Shadow then finishes his sandwiches in silence, then places the container that they came in and places it back into his cloak. He then pulls out the orthrus fang and just looks it over, just thinking about all the craziness he experienced just traveling to this city. Wondering if Tai made it out of that fog alright. After reminiscing for a bit he puts the fang back into his cloak.

Shadow then pulls out his new sword to inspect it, trying to get a handle on his new sword. He wants to be somewhat used to this sword before having to use it for real. After finishing some practice with his new sword he rests both his sword and cloak on the chair and walks over to the bed. He then pulls out the skill scroll he got from the shop earlier. Since he put it away quickly after getting it Shadow didn't notice that the scroll has a weird feel to it. It somehow feels both like paper and leather at the same time. This realization confuses him for a second but then he brushes it off, thinking that's just how the scrolls are made and that it was free, so no point in complaining now. He then sits on the bed crossed-legged with his back to the wall and opens the scroll.

Shadow sees what is written down without being able to read most of it. Then a dark light shines from it and when it finishes the scroll is blank. He's at first confused, then the skill appears in his mind.

So that's how they learn skills down here. Huh, that's convenient I guess, thinks Shadow. With everything taken care of, Shadow relaxes against the wall and decides to try and take a short nap. He goes in and out of consciousness for a little over an hour trying to get as much rest as he can. Then all of a sudden a loud crash can be heard and the room starts to shake. A siren can also be heard, though the audio seems a bit off. Shadow sees a lot of purple light can be seen coming from the uncovered parts of the window. He pulls his mask back down and quickly looks out of his window and sees three dragons causing a mess outside. He can even hear some faint screams in the distance from where the dragons are located.

What the hell, there are dragons in hell too. Then again with the creatures I've run into today I guess I shouldn't be surprised. Maybe I should leave it, but what if they come towards here? Also what if all of this chaos they're causing makes it harder to leave the city in the morning? Maybe I should just deal with it real quick, it does seem to be causing a problem, thinks Shadow, grabbing his cloak and sword.

He opens the window and quickly jumps out and heads to the dragon via the roofs so as to not be seen, as he's not sure if they are really a problem or if he's just misunderstanding the situation. Little does he know he's going to be helping Lina when he gets to them.

Lina Teaches a Lesson

To go back a bit, as Shadow leaves the table and goes upstairs Lina continues eating. As soon as Shadow is out of sight, the leader from the group of hunters there slams his fist down and starts yelling at the server at their table.

"WHAT IN HELL DO YOU MEAN YOU'RE OUT OF ROASTED IMP!?" yells the lead hunter.

The server, shaking out of fear, explains to them that the woman eating at the other table, who is Lina, actually ordered the last of what they had currently had in stock. After hearing that he looks at Lina, who is eating what he wanted to order. Seeing this he gets up and walks up to Lina's table. Lina however isn't paying him any attention, even when he gets right next to her. Seeing that she's ignoring him adds to his anger and he slams his fist onto the table.

"HEY, LOOK AT ME DAMN IT, YOU STUPID GLUTTO-NOUS BITCH!" yells the lead hunter.

Lina gives a slight sigh and puts her food down. "Yes, what do you need, and is that language and attitude necessary?" asks Lina while wiping her mouth with a napkin and refusing to look at the devil.

"Yeah there's a problem, you took the last of my food," says the lead hunter.

"Huh, that's funny, I don't see your name on any of the food that I ordered. Not that I know or care what your name is. Especially with how rude and immature you are," responds Lina.

Getting more irritated, the hunter slams his fist down onto the table again. This time though Lina's drink gets knocked over, almost landing onto her food. This makes Lina react without thinking and punch the hunter in the gut. This pushes him back so much that he falls over onto his back halfway between the two tables that Lina is sitting at and where the rest of the hunters party sits. Seeing this the two that were hanging on to him before get up rush over to him and see that he was knocked out from the punch. The party member wearing the mask however doesn't move from their original spot. They didn't even look at their party members but instead at Lina who was wiping down the table. The shield hunter picks up their unconscious leader and starts walking to the door. The archer orders their masked member to pay and then follow them. As they do, the masked member doesn't take their eyes off Lina, who resumes eating her meal. While all of this happens Lina never notices the hunter isn't next to her or that they already left. The server comes by her table with a new drink for Lina.

"Here, have this new drink on the house as both an apology and a thank-you for what just happened," says the server.

Lina stops eating and gives a confused look to the server while they swap out the cups. "A thank-you for what? Also where'd that annoying group go?" asks Lina.

"Huh, you knocked their leader out and they left," responds the server.

"Really, I was just trying to move him out of the way so I could wipe down the table before it got on my food. I didn't even hit him that hard. At least I think I didn't. Well either way it wasn't a big deal and thanks for the new drink," says Lina as she resumes eating.

After finishing her meal Lina looks over at the stairs and sees that Shadow still hasn't come back down from his room. Suddenly she feels something coming from upstairs. The feeling is the slight energy output from a skill scroll being used. Lina figures that Shadow used the scroll he got from the shop earlier. She's a bit disappointed that she didn't get to see what skill he got but shrugs it off, figuring that she can ask Shadow about it later if she is still curious. She pays for her food, grabs her bag, and then leaves the building for a bit to go walk around the city. As she leaves she notices that the thawb-wearing devil is also leaving the inn. Lina, unlike Shadow, didn't realize that there was a third party also eating there since they didn't really stand out to her, as well as her just being too hungry to care. She also feels like they seem familiar, but can't put her finger on it. The thawb devil starts jogging away from the inn.

Huh, maybe they're trying to get some after-meal exercising done before it gets too dark or something. Ah well, that's none of my business. Speaking of which I need to start heading to the gate. Hopefully the coast will be clear by now, thinks Lina as she begins walking.

It's now sunset and there are less devils out than there were earlier. Most that are still out are closing up their businesses, heading home or to an inn, and/or heading to a pub to relax. Lina just takes all of this in but focuses on heading to a specific part of the city. She heads to where the base of Pride is and checks out the gate. She can see a couple of guards in front, much to Lina's irritation.

Damn, they're still there. How long are they going to stay? I thought their shifts had ended by now. I guess I'll have to come back later then. I need to see him directly and I don't feel like having a lot of witnesses seeing me go in, thinks Lina.

Lina decides to walk away, choosing to come back in a bit to check on the gate. She decides to take some backstreets and alleys to make sure others don't see her coming directly from Pride's base. After a bit she can tell she is being followed. It seems to be a small group of devils. She wants to make sure it isn't just a coincidence so she starts making random turns through the allies and sure enough she is still being followed. After confirming this she decides to confront them by making a turn and hiding right next to the wall to catch them off guard and confront them. As soon as she does they make the turn, only for them to see that she is right in front of them. Lina confronts them only to see they are devils she met earlier. Even though she didn't get a good look at all the members of the party she remembers there were four, but now there's a fifth member. The new member is the devil she and Shadow saw before they went into the shop and then the inn. Lina wonders why they're with them. Did they just join them or were they a member the whole time? She isn't sure which one it is, but quickly stops thinking about it, as she sees it not really mattering, and confronts their leader.

"What in hell are you doing following me? Geez, are you still upset about the food back at the inn? It was just some food. Can't you just let it go?" asks Lina.

The leader brushes the hair near his face away, trying to look cool. "No, this has nothing to do with the food. In fact I'm over it now. I simply just want to give you the great honor of joining the warrior level party the Coal Diamonds, led by me, the great warrior level hunter Cole. So what do you say, ready to upgrade? I assume that your answer will be yes," says Cole smugly.

"Huh," responds Lina, looking dumbfounded by what he just said.

Cole sees this and gets thrown off a bit, but tries to play it off. "Oh I get it, my offer made you speechless. Well I can't say I'm surprised. I'm such a big deal after all. I mean I was trained by the legendary swordswoman Eve. I'm seen as the pride and joy of the entire Envy territory. I can even kill a dragon with only one attack. I'm so great in fact that I'm planning to challenge Pride just to have a fight with someone on my level," exclaims Cole smugly while flipping his hair again.

Fuck, I didn't think I would run into one of these fakes so soon after meeting a real student of hers. To make matters worse he's from my territory. This is just so embarrassing being near him. If the others hear about him I will be mocked for the next century, thinks Lina.

Cole see's that she's becoming uncomfortable and misreads the reason for this. He once again brushes away the hair near his face, thinking it makes him look cool, and looks at Lina. "Oh, are you unsure what to do? Are you thinking about that reaper-looking loser with that cheap sword that was sitting with you back at the inn? Just leave him and tell him to screw himself. I'm clearly the better choice compared to anyone else. These four here understood that and joined me," says Cole.

Whether they wanted to or not, thinks Cole.

Cole proceeds to introduce his members in order to convince Lina to join him. "My archer left her fiancé to join me because she could easily tell that I was the better choice, while my shield abandoned his family because he knew he could make more money with me than working for his family. This little pack mule with the mask back there was bought while in the Greed territory. Every great party needs a slave to carry everything for you. Finally this one with the halberd just joined, but was very determined to follow me when I told him who I was. As you can see I can get what and who I want to join my team so just stop overthinking it and just say yes already," says Cole, gaining a more sinister look on his face while still trying to act smug while brushing away his hair from his face one last time.

Lina sighs at his stupidity. During all of this she got a good look at Cole and his party members. Other than the slave and new member the rest are wearing armor that looks like it's high quality. With a closer look she can tell it's just average which probably explains the excessive number of weapons to compensate. Being done talking to this idiot she looks at Cole straight in the eyes with an irritated look. "First I'm not leaving my party with that man you saw at the inn. Next even if I did I wouldn't join a fake wannabe like you that's clearly more talk than action. Also I feel bad for your teammates that joined your party under the guise of your lie of being Eve's student. If you really were her student I wouldn't have knocked you out without even noticing. Finally, why in hell do you constantly keep messing with your hair when you talk? Just get it cut if it's bothering you that much," says Lina in an annoyed tone.

Lina turns around and begins walking away, feeling the conversation to be over. Cole starts getting furious over what she said. The archer and shield members start whispering to each other over what Lina said about Cole lying. The new recruit and masked member say nothing, but keep their eyes on Lina and Cole. In a fit of rage Cole punches the wall, leaving a small indent, and the two shut up immediately. *This bitch, who does she think she is? Not only brushing me off, but then insulting me like that in front of my members. That's it, I tried to be nice, but she's going to be mine whether she wants to or not,* thinks Cole.

"Slave, to my side now!" exclaims Cole.

The masked member gets over to him. Cole forces them to both turn around and kneel so he can dig through the bag. After a few seconds of looking he finds what he is looking for, a slave mask. The archer and shield members are shocked to see that Cole has one of these. They want to say something about it, but stop before letting out a peep. They realize they don't have much room to criticize him at this point. They've already done things that they aren't fully proud of while a part of this party, but since they have been convinced that their leader is as great as he boasted they believe it was right. So the two of them stay where they are since they still believed in who he said he was and that this is all ok. Their new member doesn't think the same way. Cole begins running toward Lina while trying to remain somewhat quiet. Just as he gets next to her he tries to wrap his arm with the mask around her. Lina sees this coming and ducks before the mask reaches her face.

Did he seriously just try to do that? That's a ballsy move to pull, especially owning those masks without a special license, which is illegal. Guess I'll just have to knock him out again and turn him in. Fuck, I still can't believe this moron is from my territory, thinks Lina while turning around while still ducked down.

Lina proceeds to stand up quickly while uppercutting Cole. The punch sends Cole flying back a bit while also dropping the mask he was holding. While Cole is down on the ground Lina picks up the mask. She inspects it and notices that something is different about this mask.

"Hey dumbass, where did you get a mask like this? I can tell this isn't a registered mask. These are illegal in every territory of hell. So how did a incompetent lying nobody like you get their hands on this?" asks Lina furiously.

Cole slouches up and arrogantly looks at Lina. "HA, they're easy to get if you know the right devils. In fact that's what I used on my pack mule slave over there. With high quality ones like that one no one can tell if it's a legal one or not when looking at it from the outside. I even have enough for the other members of my party if they had refused to join me willingly or if they get too full of themselves. I'm the best. I should get who and what I want by default!" arrogantly exclaims Cole.

The archer and tank members are just standing there in shock from what they just heard Cole say. Lina sees this, then looks back at Cole and just sighs at him because his delusional and stupid attitude is very familiar to her. Knowing he won't change, she can't just threaten him and hope he'll change. All she can do now is resolve this issue before it escalates even more. Since he's still lying on the ground she kicks him hard in the face to knock him out. She is successful in knocking him out, but she also ends up knocking out some of his teeth by mistake as well.

Whoops, I guess I kicked him too hard. I guess I should've dialed it back a bit. I used the same amount of strength needed to fight imps by mistake. Ah well, too late to worry about it now. Plus he was a huge asshole even by hell's standards. Maybe that's why Shadow went to his room while I was eating. He might've been able to tell this guy was trouble and wanted to avoid dealing with him. Anyway, better deal with his groupies before they do something, thinks Lina.

As Lina turns over to deal with the rest of the party she sees they're already dealt with. It seems that the archer and tank were taken out and tied up and gagged by their new member. Lina gives a confused look to the devil, thinking they were a part of his group.

"Thanks for distracting them, it made their capture far easier. Though it's not like they gave much of a fight to begin with. So how's about you tie up their idiot leader and we take them to the bounty office? Their team has a pretty decent bounty," says the thawb devil, tossing Lina some rope to tie up Cole.

Lina ties him up, grabs his knocked-out teeth, picks him up onto her shoulder and walks over to the other members of his team. The thawb devil is impressed that she can carry him on one shoulder with such ease. He then points down the alley past Lina. "They moved their location recently, but I walked by there earlier. If we go this way we should get there in a few minutes easily," says the thawb devil.

Lina nods and gestures to the devil to lead the way. Knowing they have been beaten and not wanting to end up like their leader, the two tied-up members walk without any resistance. The masked member also follows them while keeping between the two groups. Within a few minutes just like he said all of them are in front of the bounty office. The bounty office is rather plain looking with barren wooden floors. Some active-bounty wanted posters of criminals are on the wall behind the counter. There's a counter in front of the wall on the opposite side from the front door with currently one worker at the counter to report to. Lastly there's a door that leads to where the criminals, money, and other miscellaneous stuff is taken when a bounty is turned in.

As soon as they all walk through the door Cole wakes up. Realizing where he is he starts wailing. Getting annoyed by his moving Lina tosses him onto the floor. With Cole now moving around as best as he can, Lina decides to instill some fear into him to get him to behave himself. She crouches down next to Cole, grabs him by his hair so that he is facing her, and Lina shows him his missing teeth. Cole is initially confused, but quickly realizes they're his when he feels around his mouth with his tongue. Cole quickly calms down, not wanting to lose more teeth.

With that matter settled the thawb devil goes over to the counter to turn them in. "Hello, these devils have been causing some trouble. We'd like to turn them in. They're known as the Coal Diamonds led by that idiot over there named Cole. Do any of these three happen to have active bounties? If not then I'd like to report that they've caused a public disturbance, started fights, intimidated residents, and worst of all have possession of illegal equipment," reports the thawb devil while handing over the illegal slave mask.

The worker writes down all of the claims that were told to them. They then pull out a book from under the counter. It's a list of active bounties that aren't on the wall. After a bit of searching the worker finds one for both Cole and his party. "Yep, there's a bounty for them. The leader of the group was already charged with public intoxication, vehicle theft, damage to public property, harassment, and allegations of possession of illegal goods. There are similar charges when looking at his party as a whole as well with the added charge of extortion. With the previous charges and what you've both told and shown me they are guilty and will be punished for their crimes. As a group their bounty is worth about five to six indium coins. Not bad, but not great as bounties go. Also would you mind having that devil with the slave mask come over here? I want to inspect it to see if it's an official one or not," says the clerk.

The slave member gets waved over to the counter by the thawb devil while the clerk walks around the counter carrying some kind of stamp they got from under the counter. When the two are next to each other the clerk takes a quick look at the mask and can quickly tell it's an unofficial mask. The clerk takes the stamp and presses it against the mask. A small light flashes and the mask falls off, with the clerk grabbing it before it falls to the ground. The tied-up archer is in shock about who it is, with everyone else except for Cole not knowing who the devil was.

Lina has a realization of who it is. "OH, are you the fiancé that she left for this dumbass wannabe?" asks Lina while pointing to all three of them.

The now unmasked devil opens his mouth to say something, then quickly closes it and only nods. He either doesn't seem to want to talk or is still being affected by the mask and can't talk at the moment. Everyone else is able to start to piece together how he got himself in this situation to begin with, though most of the devils in the room really don't want to say it out loud, except for the thawb devil.

"So what, after your fiancé left you you chased their party down to get her back? Then Cole here took advantage of an opportunity in Greed's territory. When you two were alone he placed that mask on you and made you a slave and he just told the other members that he bought you. Is that basically what happened?" asks the thawb devil.

The room goes quiet from the awkwardness. After a few seconds the unmasked devil gestures that his explanation was basically what happened. The room returns to being mostly quiet from the awkwardness, with some sound coming from the archer that was formerly his fiancée fighting back a mental breakdown. The clerk clears their throat to try and get things back on track.

"Anyways since they have bounties on their heads I can take them. I will strip them of their equipment and sort through it. After ensuring that there's no more illegal equipment in their possession I will let you have your pick of what they have for yourself. Anything you don't take I will take storage of and pay you two the difference. Now if you could, could you pick them up so that I can take them to the back to be stripped and placed into cells?" asks the clerk while walking back and carrying the party's pack.

The thawb devil picks up the tied-up members and takes them over to the counter. The clerk is already sorting out the equipment from the pack to search for other illegal goods. Lina sees this with some concern. "Uh, should you be really doing that out here? Isn't there a room in the back you should do that in? Also shouldn't you strip and lock them up first before going through their pack?" asks Lina.

Without missing a beat and while still inspecting and sorting the equipment, the clerk says, "First, there was a room that we used, but it currently is unavailable due to some explosive goods one bounty had. So for the time being we have to do this out here on the counter. Not the best place, but our options are limited. Second, they have a lot of stuff so I'm getting started on it real quick before I deal with them. It's going to take a while either way. I understand your concern, but there's not much that can be done about it at this time," responds the clerk.

As soon as the clerk says that the tied-up party is at the counter. The clerk takes the last thing they grabbed out of the pack and places it on the counter and turns to them, grabbing them by the ropes and taking them to the back room. Before closing the door the clerk looks back at the three of them and says, "DON'T TOUCH ANYTHING."

The three of them only nod while the door closes. With the door finally closed the thawb devil goes to the unmasked devil and places a hand on his shoulder. "I'm sorry you had to go through all that because that guy was a jackass. You can have the first pick of the equipment and I'll split part of the reward to help you get back home," says the thawb devil.

"What the fuck, who gave you permission to decide that! Though I do agree, don't just decide that for yourself," exclaims Lina in irritation.

The thawb devil turns his head to her and says, "If you agree, why are you so mad about it then? Why does it matter in the end?"

"Because, you moron, since we took them out and turned them in together we should both agree on something like this. Otherwise you're no better than that group of assholes we just turned in," exclaims Lina, still irritated.

The unmasked devil nods to agree with Lina, leaving the thawb devil in an awkward situation. "Ok fine, I'm sorry I did that without consulting you. Also if you're going to yell at me at least use my name. It's Silt, what about you?" asks Silt.

"It's Lina, and I'm sorry I yelled at you," apologizes Lina, calming down.

With everything settled down some rustling can be heard from the back room along with some yelling. The three of them ignore it, thinking it a normal response to what's happening. All of a sudden Cole comes bursting out of the back room without his armor and other equipment. The three are in shock and Lina, who is the farthest away from the counter, moves to the front door to block it in case Cole's trying to make an escape. Meanwhile Silt charges after him to grab him while the unmasked devil runs to the pack instead. Lina sees this and wonders for a second why and then realizes what they're doing. She tries to warn Silt about what Cole probably plans to do and starts running toward the pack. Unfortunately before she can either say something or get to the bag Cole reaches it and starts digging through it. As he's doing that the clerk comes through the door as well and charges towards Cole. Lina and the unmasked devil grab the bag and pull it off the counter. As they do Cole pulls out a strange-looking whistle made of stone and bone. After pulling it out Cole is immediately tackled by both Silt and the clerk. Just before they hit the ground Cole blows the whistle, which lets out a weird fart-like noise. The clerk and Silt are confused by this and let out a small chuckle at both the noise and see this as a pathetic last attempt of escape. On the other hand both Lina and the unmasked devil are freaking out. Lina gets angry at the three of them and stares daggers at them.

"WHAT IN HELL!? Why did you let him blow that, and you, DO YOU have any idea what you have just done?!" asks Lina in an angered voice.

"Oh course I do, why else would I have blown it? Since there's no point in me staying in this city anymore I might as well have it destroyed. I'll make sure that all of you are the first taken out," says Cole arrogantly.

Silt is becoming more confused by all of this. "Wait, did I miss something? All this idiot did was blow a whistle that made a fart sound. What's so dangerous about that?" asks Silt.

"You're the idiot here Silt. I know they're rare, but have you never heard of those whistles before? The fart noise is just a leftover sound only caused after performing its real purpose, summoning dragons!" exclaims Lina.

Dragons and Sins

Silt and the clerk become dumbfounded by what they just heard. It's true that there are rumors of some rare items that can summon beasts, but it's hard to believe that a whistle could summon dragons. Even more unbelievable that someone like Cole could get his hands on one. Though seeing how serious Lina is about the situation it's better to trust her than take that risk. They now see Cole trying to blow the whistle again. Now knowing what it does they quickly knock it out of his hand, though it is too late because as soon as the whistle hits the floor several roars can be heard. Lina quickly runs outside and sees three pride dragons already hovering above the city. The three dragons consist of two wyverns being led by a violet colored pride dragon. They are constantly moving their heads to get a good scope of the area as if they're looking for a place safe to land. Everyone else runs out with the clerk holding on to Cole in a choke hold. Silt just looks at them in both fear and confusion as this is his first time seeing these creatures.

"WHAT IN HELL ARE THOSE?!" asks Silt with great frisson.

Lina, trying to remain calm, looks over to him. "They're known as pride dragons. They're creatures basically made out of pure pride energy. Normally each territory only has about one dragon created from remnants of their sin energy, but this territory is special. Since the former Pride destroyed all of the gems of every town and village in her territory she let out giant waves of pride energy and created a dragon with each one destroyed. Normally they stay away from settlements with a sin gem. That is unless some dumbass blows an illegal whistle that summons them to the area it's been blown in. Also, for the record, they're one of if not the strongest wild beast demons in hell. It usually takes someone as powerful as a sin to kill them," says Lina, getting somewhat irritated near the end.

Silt calms down from the initial shock and turns his head toward Lina. "Wait what, are they really that powerful? Then shouldn't the new Pride get rid of them? This is both his city and territory after all. Also why aren't we hearing screams from around the city?" asks Silt.

"He probably needs time to prepare. They did just show up out of nowhere thanks to this idiot. Also I doubt many have seen them yet. Most devils are somewhere eating, drinking, or sleeping by this point. They also don't have much reason to look up around this time anyways. Though once the alarms go off and they finally are spotted it's going to be chaos. Which is kind of an ironic thing to say," says Lina.

"Speaking of the alarm, shouldn't it have gone off when they entered the city?" asks the clerk.

Lina becomes even more worried because the clerk has a point. She looks at the dragons, still hovering until they finally pick a spot to land. "Maybe they are still damaged from when the former Pride was in charge. I heard that she did get them to send messages throughout the city to insult and order the men around. Maybe that's why we haven't heard it yet," says Lina while giving an awkward and uncomfortable laugh.

As the dragons start to descend Silt looks at them with newfound vigor. "Well it seems that Pride wants to take his damn time doesn't he. Hm, who knows, maybe he's too busy to take care of them or maybe he just can't. I mean if he's not going to do anything then I guess I'll have to step up. I'm sure I could handle at least one of them. Those dragons have to have a weak point somewhere. I just need to find it," says Silt, getting both excited and a little arrogant.

Lina regains some composure and looks back at Silt. "Don't be a reckless idiot like the moron that summoned them. Pride's probably already on this matter. Though to be honest he might not know the proper way to kill them without taking part of the city with him," responds Lina, holding back the urge to smack him.

"Wait what the fuck, take out part of the city? Do these things explode or something when they die or if they're not killed the right way?" asks Silt.

"Well yes and no, it's just that a sin can take them out but the normal method would cause a powerful explosion in order to destroy them. There's a method to do it in a settlement, but I don't know if he was taught it yet," answers Lina.

"Wait a second there, as far as I'm aware there hasn't been a confirmed killing of a dragon in a few centuries and even then it wasn't even killed by a sin. So how do you know that the sins have different ways to handle dragons depending on if they're in a settlement or not? Also how would you know if he wasn't taught it yet exactly?" asks Silt with the clerk still holding on to Cole and nodding in agreement.

Lina begins to panic and tries to change the subject. "Uh, hey wait, we should brace for impact when the dragons land and the ground shakes, not to mention the slight shock wave that will pass through," says Lina in a panicked tone.

It's clear that she is both trying to change the subject and right about the dragons' landing. Sure enough the dragons' landing causes the ground to shake. The shock wave from their landing causes nearby windows to shatter. As soon as they land an alarm finally goes off, but sounds somewhat choppy, as if it was fixed in a hurry. With most devils in surprise at what happened and now hearing the alarm, they look to see what happened and see the dragons. As Lina said the devils start to panic. They begin running away, leaving their homes and establishments out of fear. Meanwhile for Lina, Silt, and the clerk, running isn't much of a viable option since one of the wyverns has landed near them and can see them if it looks in their direction and running could draw its attention. The best option they can do right now is hide and try to get away the first chance there's an opening.

All of a sudden Cole begins to laugh. "See this is what happens when you oppose me. These dragons will go about destroying every-thing. Tell me clerk, do you think that you can keep hold of me and run away from this danger? That whistle not only summons them but also makes them obligated to locate and obey me. You four will be nothing but snacks for them once they figure out my location. Then with you idiots taken care of I can order them to die and take credit as a slayer of dragons. My reputation will soar. Who knows, I might even be made into a sin and replace those two worthless sins that haven't unlocked their real power yet. Hm, now which sin sounds better to me: Lust or Envy?" says Cole with great arrogance.

Lina gets furious at what he said and punches him in the face. "You fucking psychopath, you would destroy a whole city just to escape capture and make yourself look good? First off there's no way a loser like you would ever become a sin even if your plan did work. Second, what about your two lackeys still tied up in the back room? They are just as likely to die from the dragon's rampage," exclaims Lina with great anger.

"Who the fuck cares about them? Those morons followed me of their own free will. Granted I tricked them, but they still followed me because I am so great. Once I take out these dragons there will be crowds of devils and monsters lining up to want to be by my side. So I can easily replace them if they do die. They are starting to reach the limits of their usefulness anyways so it is time to trade up," says Cole, still with great arrogance.

The clerk then tightens their hold on Cole. "Don't treat others' lives as something to throw away for your own gain. If you keep talking like that I'll just slit your throat and kill you before the dragons can find you," says the clerk, pulling out a knife and placing it near Cole's neck.

As soon as he does that though one of the wyvern locates them and roars to call for the other two. Within a matter of seconds the other wyvern and the leading dragon surround them. Cole just laughs more, knowing that three of them are dead. *Fuck, I guess I have no choice now. If Yuki isn't going to come and deal with them. I have to take care of them myself. Dammit, I really didn't want to have to reveal my secret until I solved my problem, but I guess I don't have that option anymore,* thinks Lina.

The dragon starts reaching one of its front claws at them. It is clear it is heading towards Cole and the clerk. Lina begins whispering a chant of some kind to herself. With the dragons surrounding them Cole and the clerk don't notice, but Silt does. *What in hell is she chanting? I thought that she was some kind of thief based on her attire and equipment. Ah fuck it I don't have time to question that right now. I doubt I'll be able to handle all three at once, so anything would be helpful right now,* thinks Silt.

As soon as the dragon's claw gets close to them Silt grabs his halberd and takes a swing at it. At that same time Lina sees this and interrupts her chant and starts a different one. The new chant is finished quickly and causes a surge of energy to form around Lina. She transfers this energy into Silt's halberd as a means to add more power into it. The halberd begins to glow with a green aura, making the weapon twice as strong, though Silt doesn't notice or care at the moment. He lands his attack on the dragon's claw between its knuckles. The attack does cut the hand, but doesn't go very deep. At best it cuts through a couple of scales. The blade of the halberd also breaks off from just the sheer amount of force that Silt put into his swing. "Huh, I guess they're tougher than I thought. I guess my weapon just couldn't cut it, literally," whispers Silt in a disappointed tone.

The dragon does retract its claw a bit though just from caution for a moment. Assuring that they aren't a threat it resumes trying to grab Cole. The clerk presses the knife closer to Cole's neck and starts to draw blood. Suddenly the dragon stops and looks behind it with the two wyverns looking in the same direction. Cole gets furious at the dragons for getting distracted. "What the fuck are you stupid dumbass giant lizards doing? Why the fuck are you getting distracted? Use those tiny brains of yours and rescue me right this fucking second!" yells Cole.

The dragons pay no mind to Cole. The clerk keeps their eyes on the dragons while covering Cole's mouth without letting go of the knife. Lina and Silt on the other hand are looking in the direction that the dragons are looking and see someone. With it getting darker out they have trouble making out who it is, but notice something that they are wearing. It is a brown cloak with an erratic pattern on it. The dragons look at them with confusion, feeling that another one of their own is standing where they stand. Silt looks at it thinking that it looks familiar, but can't put his finger one it. Lina however instantly recognizes it and knows that it's Shadow. "Perfect, with Shadow here this situation is basically solved now. I'm sure that outside of a sin he's the only one that can take care of them," says Lina. *I'm glad he showed up when he did. I really didn't want to have to reveal my secret until I resolved my problem,* thinks Lina.

Seeing that Lina is familiar with the new contender Silt remembers that it was the other member that she was with earlier at both the inn and outside the shop. Though not knowing his skills Silt wonders if Lina should be so confident in Shadow. "Hey, are you sure this guy is as good as you say? I mean my halberd could only cut a few scales before breaking. Are you sure that this guy with his sword can really handle them?" asks Silt.

As soon as Silt asks this however the dragons start reaching out for Shadow. They seem to be getting ready to attack him, but Shadow appears to be unfazed by this. Shadow places his left hand over where his eyes would be behind his mask. The four on the ground stand there in confusion as to why he did this.

What in hell is that guy doing, thinks the clerk.

Is he that confident that he'll win that he's covering his eyes for more of a challenge? thinks Silt.

Shadow, just what are you doing? This is no time for jokes, thinks Lina.

Ha, so that idiot just showed up just to accept his fate and die, thinks Cole.

Geez, the aura coming off the dragons is so strong I can barely see. It's like staring directly at a bright lightbulb. I also need to be careful. I can see the auras of others down there. I can't just go swinging my sword around like an idiot. If I hurt them or break something they could easily get me in trouble. They might even think I had something to do with this. I should just handle this and run back quickly, thinks Shadow.

As the claw gets closer he grabs his sword with his right hand while his left is still covering his eyes to help him see. The claw is now next to Shadow. It's so close that Shadow can even feel the body heat from it. As soon as it gets close to him though the claw suddenly drops onto the roof, with Shadow now standing on it. Everyone is dumbfounded until they see that the claw is actually cut off at the wrist. Shadow, with his sword drawn in his right hand and his eyes shaded with his left, leaps at the dragon. With one slash from his sword the dragon's head is severed from its body. Without missing a beat Shadow lands onto the bounty building and jumps at one of the wyverns. It also gets decapitated, with Shadow jumping off its body and heading to the other wyvern. Its fate is the same as the others, with Shadow jumping off this wyvern to jump back to the roof he started from. As soon as Shadow lands back onto the first roof the head of the dragon finally hits the ground and the body slumps over the building. The same happens with the wyverns moments later. *Hm, compared to the orthrus earlier, that was far easier. Then again this time I had a weapon, so it's not a fair comparison,* thinks Shadow.

Shadow looks down to see if everyone is alright. He notices Lina down there as well as Silt and Cole, remembering them only as those devils back at the inn as he doesn't know their names. He also notices two others that he doesn't recognize. Shadow becomes quite nervous, even more than with the dragons. Especially since one of the new faces is even holding Cole by the neck and that it is bleeding somewhat. He even notices that Cole has started going limp and what looks like tears are falling to the ground. *Why is he being held by his neck? Why is he bleeding? Was he hurt or did they hurt him? Is that why he's crying? What have they been doing to him? Also where are the other members* of his party that I saw at the inn? Is that other devil that I haven't seen before the one with the slave mask from earlier? If so, what about the others? Were they killed by the dragons before I got here? thinks Shadow, becoming more nervous and paranoid with each question.

Lina gestures to Shadow to come down so she can fill him in on what he's missed. Unfortunately Shadow has become so nervous about them that he sees her gesture as something else. *Why is she telling me to come down? Are they upset that I took so long to get here? Maybe she plans to have the other two attack me as soon as I jump down. Maybe that was her plan the whole time. Though she seems nice and harmless enough. Maybe she just wants me to come down just to talk. Hm, then again I know from past experiences that people that act like that at first are the most dangerous. I probably shouldn't take a chance right now. I should just run back to my room at the inn quickly and block my door more just in case. If Lina does want to tell me something she could always just do it through the door back at the inn or in the morning,* thinks Shadow.

Shadow sheaths his sword and runs back in the direction he came from. This actually confuses everyone else on the ground along with an awkward silence. Lina just sighs and rubs the back of her head. *I guess I shouldn't be surprised at this point. I think I'm starting to get an idea of his personality. I'll just have to talk with him back at the inn,* thinks Lina.

Silt decides to cut through the awkward silence and speak up. "Ok, What in hell was that all about? The guy comes out of nowhere, kills three dragons in a matter of seconds and then leaves. What's up with that?" asks Silt, with both the unmasked devil and the clerk slightly nodding in agreement.

"From what I know from my limited time spent with him I can tell you that he's more of a loner. Either that or he has trouble trusting others for some reason or another," says Lina while giving a slight shrug.

With the calm now restored they all start hearing the sound of someone crying coming from the clerk's direction. The other three look over and see Cole who has started both going limp and crying. They can tell it's because his last attempt to escape just failed. With both Silt and the unmasked devil feeling joyous seeing him cry like this, Lina feels different. She wants to kick him more now that he is at his lowest point. So she walks over to the clerk and grabs on to Cole's shoulder tightly. "You can let go of him now. I'll make sure he doesn't make a run for it. You three should head back inside to make sure everything is still in one piece and also check on the others in the back and make sure they are ok and still locked up," says Lina while not taking her eyes off Cole.

The clerk agrees and releases their hold on Cole. Without the support from being held Cole falls slightly, but is still being held up by Lina. The clerk heads back inside with the other two not far behind. With Lina and Cole now alone Lina gets close to Cole's ear. "That guy just now that killed those dragons, he's a real student of Eve, unlike you," whispers Lina with a smug look on her face.

Cole processes what she told him. What little bit of fight that is left in him now leaves. His eyes are empty and show barely any signs of life. His spirit is essentially broken. Silt comes back out of the building and looks at the two of them.

"Hey, everything is still in order, just some broken glass and fallen things from the shock wave. Even the prisoners in the back stayed put despite everything that was going on. Apparently all that commotion knocked some of the cell doors open so they could have made a break for it, though I doubt that. Even though they could, they probably would still just stay put rather than deal with dragons. Well anyways, the clerk asked me to come back out and fetch this guy. They also want to know what to do about the dragon corpses. They'll definitely catch a great price, but the guy that killed them didn't stick around. We aren't sure how to deal with this. I mean I wouldn't mind the money, but I don't want to steal credit. Plus they're huge and it's going to be tough getting them through the city to the nearest butcher," says Silt.

"Oh, well there isn't much we can do about the former until both things calm down and the sun rises. The latter however should be much easier since I know the guy," says Lina, handing over Cole.

"Oh, you do now? Then you must introduce me to him later. Also I will be taking those dragons off of your hands, so don't worry your little heads about it," says an unknown voice.

Lina and Silt are caught off guard by this and try to figure out who said it. Lina looks above them and sees three devils on the roof of the building in front of the bounty building. Silt also looks up to see them and sees three devils wearing robes to hide their identities, though he does notice that the two on the side are also wearing slave masks. The masks are that of a rabbit and a fox. However Lina is more focused on the one in the middle since she recognized his voice. She wants to be sure so she gets a good look at him. She sees a fit man with slightly shaggy black hair with a streak of purple in it. He's dressed in what seems to be formal dark gray pants, black shoes, and a white button-down shirt. After getting a good look Lina is sure of it. It's the new sin of pride, Yuki. As soon as she recognizes him Yuki snaps his fingers and the two wearing masks disappear from sight. Lina quickly looks over to the dragons and sees them there picking up the corpses of the two wyverns with relative ease, with them disappearing again, only this time taking the wyverns with them. Then within a matter of seconds they reappear and grab the pride dragon. With it being larger they have some slight issues lifting it, but still pick it up, though with more effort then before.

Silt, angered by what's happening, drops Cole to fall to the ground and leaps at the two of them in an attempt to stop them. He moves at them with tremendous speed closing the distance between them in only a second. He prepares to punch one of them using both his strength and momentum. He aims for the one with the rabbit mask first since they are closer. As soon as he is arms length away from the rabbit he throws his punch, though the rabbit-masked devil blocks it with their arm with only some slight movement. The rabbit then pushes back and sends Silt flying back to where he started, actually landing on top of Cole, Cole not caring that he is being stood on. This leaves Silt both confused and more enraged by how easily they were able to both block his punch and knock him back.

"Don't bother trying to fight my attendants. It's clear that you are not even close to their level. Maybe if you were able to do more then break a few scales you might have some promise. Though then again you needed help just to do that much," says Yuki as he looks at both Silt and Lina.

"Hmph, so you the title of pride isn't just for show. You really are one prideful arrogant bastard," says Silt.

"Ha, your insults mean very little to me. I'm far above someone like you," scoffs Yuki.

"Oh get off your high horse. You're just one of seven sins," responds Silt.

"I'm not just a sin. I AM A GOD!" yells Yuki while stretching out his arms and bending back as to look down his nose at Silt. His declaration is so loud that it's echoing through the alley.

With saying that the two masked attendants leave with the pride dragon. Yuki positions himself back to normal and looks over at Lina with a slight confusion as to why she was here. *Why in hell is she here? Did she want to talk with me about something? She did say that she knows the man that killed the dragons. Is she looking over him or something? Maybe it's a new attendant for her. No, then he wouldn't have just left after killing the dragons. Aw well, I'll just have her bring him over tomorrow and ask them,* thinks Yuki.

Yuki walks over to Lina and leans close to her ear so that only she can hear what he has to say. "Bring that man over to my home. I want to thank him for taking care of those dragons for me as well as pay him for his services. I also want to ask both of you a few questions, one of which is why you are here in the first place without prior notice? I expect both of you over soon," says Yuki before disappearing.

Silt sees this while still standing on Cole and wonders what is going on between the two of them. After Yuki leaves, Lina sees Silt staring at her. "What?" asks Lina.

"What do you mean, 'what'? What was the sin of pride whispering to you? What did he tell you and only you? Are you hiding something? I remember how you seem to know a lot of stuff about how to handle the dragons. There was also that weird chanting that you were doing. Just who in hell are you?" asks Silt.

"Um, well you see uh," says Lina.

Before Lina can say any more the clerk comes out of the door and says to the two of them, "Just how long are the two of you planning on making me wait? Stop standing on him and bring that criminal in already.."

Lina and Silt realize that they had completely forgotten about him. They both then look at Cole who is still under Silt's feet. He's still conscious, but hasn't even tried to make an escape, believing it to be pointless. Silt steps off of Cole and picks him back up.

"Do you have any idea what that noise a minute ago was? It sounded like someone was saying something, but I couldn't make it out. Also what happened to the dragons?" asks the clerk.

"The sin of pride came and took them. He said he'd handle the payment for their corpses. Also that noise was just him yelling at something I said," responds Silt.

The clerk seems surprised, but remembering what just happened, it's not out of the realm of possibility. They calm down, and then just nod and gesture to them to come inside. The two begin to walk to the door, but before they enter Silt looks at Lina. "After we're finished here we're going to continue our talk. I still want my answers," says Silt as he walks through the door with Cole.

Lina gulps at this, knowing she's put herself in a bad situation. *Crap, I really don't want to reveal everything. The truth is too embarrassing. Maybe he won't believe me. No, that ship sailed when Yuki showed up. If I didn't use up most of my energy with those spells I could just knock him out. My best bet now is to sneak away immediately after getting the reward,* thinks Lina as she walks through the door.

Inside Silt hands Cole over to the clerk. The clerk grabs him and begins to head to the back room. Before going through the door he leaves the reward money on the counter and looks back at them. "I already sorted through his equipment while you two took your time coming back in. Pick what you want from it and whatever's left will be compensated for," says the clerk, taking Cole to the back room. The two look over the equipment which consists of weapons, clothing, jewelry, and other miscellaneous items. Lina doesn't see anything of interest from the pile at first, then notices an interesting set of wrist amulets. They are both made of metal with a dark gem of some type placed in the middle. They have a black base color with a gray pattern covering them, coming from the gem. She picks them up to inspect them closer and quickly realizes what they can do. *Are you serious, that idiot had these and didn't use them? What, did he think they weren't flashy enough to wear or something? Hm, then again maybe he didn't know what they do since they aren't flashy. Granted they aren't high quality, but it sure would've been more useful than fucking dragons. Well either way this will make things a lot easier for me,* thinks Lina. "I'll only take these, nothing else interests me," says Lina, equipping the armbands.

Silt looks over to her and only nods. He then looks over to the unmasked devil. "Hey, is any of this stuff yours?" asks Silt.

The unmasked devil nods to Silt. He looks to Silt and says, "Yes, when I was forcibly made into his slave he took any equipment that I had on me. Most of it's still here thankfully."

"Then come and grab them before the clerk comes back. Don't worry, nothing in this pile really interests me," says Silt, with Lina nodding in agreement.

The devil walks up to the counter and grabs what equipment was his, which includes a few sets of clothes, and a falcata sword. After getting everything he backs away and bows in thanks. Silt and Lina only nod back in response. As that happens the clerk returns from the back room. "So have you all picked everything from the pile? If so I can take it and calculate the payment for compensation," says the clerk.

The three nod to the clerk. With that the clerk looks at what is left and quickly calculates the amount. They then grab everything and head to the back room once more. While the clerk is in the back room the room with everyone else is filled with an awkward silence. No one has anything to say. In this silence Silt looks over to Lina almost like he's staring her down. Lina can feel that Silt is starting to get impatient and wants to have that talk. This only leaves Lina more uncomfortable as she puts on her new wrist amulets. Finally the clerk returns again after a few minutes. "Ok, with their bounty and the compensation of their leftover goods your payment comes out to eight indium coins," says the clerk.

Lina nods in thanks and quickly walks up to the counter and grabs two of them. While the other two both grab three each of what remains Lina starts heading for the door. The other two thank the clerk and Silt immediately starts going after Lina with the unmasked devil following not far behind. Lina isn't able to get far before Silt grabs her shoulder, keeping her from trying to run away. Though before Silt can say anything the unmasked devil clears his throat. "Sorry, but before you have your important conversation I just wanted to take this opportunity to properly thank you for saving me. I really appreciate the two of you for that and putting that psycho behind bars. Until you two I feared that I'd spend the rest of my life as his slave while he continued to commit crimes behind everyone's backs and pretended to be a great hunter," says the unmasked devil while bowing in thanks.

Lina pats their shoulder and the trio start walking away from the bounty building. "No problem, given his personality it was only a matter of time before he and his groupies got caught anyways. Just be more careful from now on. There are more devils that do the same thing only they're smart enough to not be super cocky and get caught. Also, try to forget about your ex-fiancé. Someone who will leave you just because someone boasted about themselves is not worth the effort. I can tell that you deserve far better. Anyways you should head back to your hometown in the morning. I'm sure there are devils worried about you. Speaking of which, do you even have a place to stay the night with your party now arrested?" says Lina, with Silt nodding in agreement.

The unmasked devil nods and responds, "Yes, it's the inn from earlier. Cole already paid for the night. So might as well not let it go to waste."

The unmasked devil walks off back to the inn they were all eating at while Silt and Lina stop walking. The unmasked devil, knowing they want to talk with each other, takes the hint and continues to walk back. Silt watches them walk off while staying close to Lina. Meanwhile Lina takes her new wrist amulets and touches their gems together. As soon as the devil is out of sight Silt starts turning to face Lina. "Ok now that we're alone tell me how you, wait WHERE IN HELL DID YOU GO?!" exclaims Silt, seeing that Lina is gone without him realizing.

Wondering where she went, Silt starts looking all around him thinking she's hiding. He then remembers what she grabbed from the pile of loot and how she tapped them together before disappearing. He quickly realizes that they aren't normal pieces of jewelry, but presence-hiding amulets. This realization proceeds to enrage Silt mostly because he didn't realize this sooner. Meanwhile Lina is making her way back to the inn while hearing Silt faintly both screaming and yelling and cursing at her for running away.

Geez, he's really mad now isn't he? I guess he really wanted to figure out who I really am. I hope I don't run into him again anytime soon, because I don't think he'll be in the mood to hear my excuses. I just need to talk with Yuki and hopefully he can help me with my situation. I should also have Shadow come along so that Yuki can give his reward. He's probably already made it back to the inn by now so I'll check his room, thinks Lina.

Lina soon makes it back to the inn. She sees the devil that she and Silt helped earlier heading up the stairs to the rooms. He turns back and sees Lina and waves to her with Lina waving back. Lina also heads up the stairs and heads to the door of Shadow's room. She proceeds to knock on the door. At first there is no answer so she knocks again. "Hey Shadow, are you back?" asks Lina as she grabs the doorknob.

As Lina starts turning the knob Shadow speaks up. "I'm here, so please don't open the door. Are you here about the dragons? Are you going to tell me that I shouldn't have killed them?" asks Shadow.

"What? No, well yes it's about the dragons, but killing them was fine. Actually the sin of pride himself even took the corpses of the dragons and told me to tell you to visit him so he can reward you," answers Lina.

It's not like I killed them for a reward. I just thought that it seemed dangerous and feared that if they weren't taken care of then it could have affected me trying to leave the city and head to the next territory. Though I don't know a lot of how things work here in hell. For all I know it was a misunderstanding on my part. It's a good thing that I was in the right and I don't seem to be in trouble for killing them, thinks Shadow.

"Also I want to thank you for helping me a second time today. I feel like it's partially my fault the dragons showed up in the first place. So in the morning I'll lead you to Pride's base so that you can get your reward. So goodnight Shadow, see you in the morning," says Lina while letting go of the knob.

"Goodnight" responds Shadow.

Hmm, I feel suspicious of how she said she would lead me to my reward. What if she's trying to lead me to a trap or an ambush instead? I don't know, Lina seems like she's nice enough, but I'm in hell and I have to be even more wary of others than normal. Maybe I should head to Pride's base once it gets fully dark out and there's little to no one else out. I can check things out first. If it's a trap or ambush I might see what they plan beforehand and find the best way to escape, thinks Shadow while sitting on top of the bed trying to get some more rest.

I'm sure he's going to try and sneak out before we go see Yuki. I can't have him try and ditch me again. Well too bad Shadow, I'm going to make sure that you meet him, even if I have to keep an eye on your room. So I better get some rest while I can. I doubt he'll try to run right now with everything still being hectic. So he'll either try to leave when it's completely dark or at dawn. It won't matter. With my new presence-hiding amulets I can follow you without you even knowing I'm there, maybe, thinks Lina as she gets back to her room right next to Shadow's.

An Unwanted Push Forward

Soon enough it's finally completely dark outside and people are going to sleep. Shadow wakes up and looks out the window and sees that the area is mostly empty now. It almost seems as if the chaos from the dragons didn't happen. Shadow collects all of his equipment, moves the furniture back to where it originally was, and leaves his room while trying to make as little noise as possible.

While it's dark I can take a look at Pride's base without others seeing me, hopefully, thinks Shadow.

Shadow leaves the inn and starts heading to the giant glow of purple energy coming from the base of Pride to check it out for later. With the sun now completely set the only thing that is helping Shadow see are the lanterns as well as the aura coming from the gems protecting the city. On the way Shadow notices a presence following him, but ignores it since he recognizes the aura and sees them as non-hostile, though he keeps his hand near his sword just in case. Shadow continues his walk to Pride's base while keeping his guard up somewhat. As he gets closer he starts noticing something strange. There are more actual trees growing from the ground, with them becoming almost like a forest the closer he gets to the base. Shadow finds this confusing, but assumes it probably is due to Pride's influence that they were able to grow without burning to a crisp. Either way it isn't something to worry about right now and so Shadow continues to the base.

As Shadow reaches Pride's base he sees a light which probably signifies the entrance for the base. As he gets closer to the light Shadow sees someone else near the entrance.

Wait, who is that? It's not Pride, is it? I doubt I'm ready to face him. Though Lina did say that he wanted to thank and compensate me for the dragons. But then again that still doesn't change that I still need to get his key. Maybe I can convince him to give it to me instead of money. Though I doubt it, thinks Shadow.

Getting closer Shadow notices that the figure is actually the devil that was the one leaving the shop earlier just before he and Lina went in, at the inn he's staying at, and with Lina during the dragon's attack. Getting a closer look, he confirms with himself that the devil in front of him is in fact wearing something called a thawb, which he remembers seeing online sometime before coming to hell. Shadow also notices that the devil doesn't seem to be carrying any weapons that he can see, which he found weird since he saw him with a halberd earlier. He also notices that most of the devil is covered by the thawb and the only part of their body that is visible is the upper part of their face. From what he can see, their skin has a peach or tan shade, though it is hard to tell with the poor lighting. Other than that, Shadow can't make out any more detail because the devil is covered by their dense purple and red aura.

The devil now notices Shadow looking at them, recognizes them, and slightly waves to him. "Hey there again, fancy seeing you here. So are you also here to take your chances against Pride? Were the dragons not enough for you or something?" asks the devil in the thawb.

By the sound of their voice Shadow is able to tell that the devil is a man, something he wasn't sure of beforehand. Shadow shakes his head. "No, I just wanted to look at the base. Apparently I was summoned here to be thanked for taking care of them. Though that's not until morning," responds Shadow, walking closer to the devil.

"Ah, getting some scouting done beforehand is not a bad idea. I can't really blame you. I mean a sin summoning you to their own base. From what I hear that rarely happens. So I get your nervousness, better to be safe than sorry. Especially with the rumor about him," says the devil in the thawb, with Shadow curious about what he said.

"What rumor?" asks Shadow.

"Just that he's far stronger when the sun is out. He becomes so strong that at his strongest point he's stronger than the other sins combined. If the rumor is to be believed," answers the thawb devil, with Shadow becoming even more nervous.

Hearing this, Shadow begins to freak out internally. *AHHH, he's stronger than the other sins. No wonder Master Eve didn't want me fighting him first. There's no way I can beat him as I am now. Especially since he wants to meet me in the morning. Does he know that I need his key and plans to take me out? No wait, then again this devil did say that they are only rumors and Lina says that Pride wants to compensate me for saving the city. For now I should try to calm down. Panicking will only make things worse,* thinks Shadow.

The two of them look at the base and see that it resembles a giant rook chess piece. The base is made from some kind of stone, though it's hard to tell what kind from the distance. The base also has a purple tint all over it, though it's hard to tell if it's the base's natural color or if it's being dyed from all the aura in the area. Behind the base there seems to be a giant purple tree seeming almost bigger than the base itself, which is what seems to be the source of the purple energy Shadow could see from all over the city. While getting closer to the base they start to be able to see into the hole surrounding the base. Looking into said hole below the base, Shadow notices the large glow of several colors. While taking a closer look he sees a possibly bottomless pit full of people, with one or more trees of varying types with unnaturally colored leaves sprouting from them, though Shadow has trouble seeing very far down due to too much light essentially blinding him. The light's coming from the strong glow of the sinner's trees basically making it as bright as day to Shadow. Their muffled screams can be heard while parts of the trees coming from them are sawed off.

Those must be the sinners under Pride's jurisdiction. Those trees must be the result of those seeds that Lina mentioned. Though why are the leaves those strange colors? The trees in the city and above the pit have normal green leaves. Hm, maybe it's because they're still attached to the sinners. I'll look into it later, thinks Shadow.

"Geez, I can barely see anything past or under the bridge," says the devil in the thawb.

Shadow hears this and remembers that not everyone has the ability to see auras like he can now. So without the auras lighting the area the only place with actual light is from the front bridge which is using those same lamps seen in the city. Because of this the two start walking in front of the bridge so that the thawb devil can see better.

"Oh, my name's Silt by the way. I kind of forgot that we never told each other our names yet. With everything going on I guess it slipped my mind. So anyways, what's your name Mr. Dragon Killer? Also, if you don't mind me asking, why do you make yourself look like a reaper with your mask?" asks Silt.

"Shadow, and personal reasons," responds Shadow while still observing the area.

"Ok Shadow, fair enough, sorry for asking if it's a touchy subject. Well anyways, it looks like that bridge is the only way in there," says Silt. Silt points to the stone bridge that is the only thing connecting the base to the ground where the two of them are standing.

"Though while going around the area earlier I did find that there does seem to be another opening on the other side. However I don't think that one will work since it seems that it's more for transporting the sinners in this territory along with their broken-off sin trees to or from the base. Even then it's more of what they'd call 'an elevator.' So with that option off the table that leaves us with only one way in or out. Though not going to lie I was kind of expecting a better form of security from a sin. I mean it was laughably easy to sneak in, even though the only viable way to get to and from the base directly is this bridge. It's not even a drawbridge or something. Anyone could get in or out if they wanted to. You'd think someone as important as a sin would do more to keep out intruders or would-be challengers like us huh," says Silt, with Shadow nodding slightly out of awkwardness.

Silt goes on about the base and such, however, Shadow has started tuning him out.

I think he might talk even more than Lina, but he has brought up some things that I can use. Well either way, I've got a good look now to head baaaa—!? thinks Shadow while being pushed from behind.

"Shadow what happeeeened?!" asks Silt while also getting pushed from behind.

Landing onto the bridge face-first they wonder who or what did that. When Shadow and Silt both look back to see who or what pushed them they see a devil covering their face with two bandanas. Shadow immediately knows it was Lina because aside from covering her face she looks exactly the same from earlier. Silt however has no idea who the devil is due to poor lighting making it hard for him to get a good look at her.

So you finally revealed yourself after following me from the inn. But why push me and Silt? Maybe you were planning to do this from the beginning, that's why you were so nice. Was what you told me about Pride wanting to compensate me for the dragons also a lie in order to lure me here? Well I'm not going to let you get your way if I can help it, thinks Shadow as he starts to walk past Lina.

"Well that was uncalled for, but if you wanted to go you could have, huh?" says Silt as he and Shadow start heading to the devil, but they are stopped by something and can't go back to where they were just standing.

An invisible wall that appeared after they fell allows them in but not out. After passing the invisible wall the sinners' screams became louder, showing that the wall also acts as a sound muffler, but Shadow notices that it still sounds quieter than it should, meaning that there's another invisible wall to act as a sound barrier over the hole directly to quiet their screams even more. Shadow looks over the side of the bridge to try and get a better look down the hole, but can't see much of anything since the light from all the sinful auras from the sinners still makes it hard to see very far down. Shadow quickly pulls away from the edge as all the light is starting to hurt his eyes. As Shadow rubs his eyes Lina walks past the wall.

"So do you mind telling us why you pushed us?" asks Silt.

Lina doesn't say anything and Silt starts to get irritated with her, still not recognizing her due to the poor lighting.

"Hey, are you going to explain yourself or are you going to try and make yourself look like the silent type to try and make yourself look cool? Because if you are, it's not working, it just makes you seem annoying," says Silt in an irritated tone, forgetting Shadow can hear him.

"HMMM, looks like I've got some uninvited visitors," says a familiar voice from further down the bridge. The three of them turn to look over and they see the sin of pride, Yuki. He's standing there on the bridge between them and the base. He has his arms crossed with his head tilted up enough so that he is slightly looking down his nose at the trio.

Crap, I guess I have no choice in avoiding Pride now. Hmm, then again, maybe I can ask him and get him to let me go because it was an accident, and Lina did say he wanted to thank me for taking out those dragons earlier. Maybe I can have him just let us leave and say we're even. All I need to do is gain his favor which should be easy enough, thinks Shadow.

Shadow slightly steps forward toward Yuki and kneels down and goes into a praying stance. "Oh great Lord Pride, we apologize for invading your home. We only wanted to admire such a wondrous home of such a great sin. It was not our intention to go past your field, but we lost our footing and came through by accident. Could a great sin such as yourself please let us out please? I was told that you wanted to thank and reward me for my assistance earlier, but there is no need. If you could just let us leave that will be enough for me," says Shadow while keeping his prayer stance.

Yuki stands there thinking it over. He also recognizes him as the one that saved the city earlier, then gets a giant grin on his face. Yuki bends backward to look down his nose more. "Normally I would refuse such an idiotic request, but since did such a nice thing for me and you clearly know your place compared to me I can let you three gooooo," says Yuki while Silt takes the opportunity to trip him while he's distracted.

WHY? We were almost out, thinks Shadow.

"Huh, that was easier than I thought. He's not that tough while stroking his ego. I guess what happened earlier was just a fluke," says Silt with some slight arrogance.

Yuki becomes incredibly angry, then gets up and then seemingly starts floating with the floor cracking under him.

"What in hell is going on here? I didn't know he could fly!" yells Silt in surprise, confusion, and slight fear.

Shadow isn't confused because he can see the truth. Yuki isn't floating, his energy is formed around his body, energy formed into the shape of an extremely buff body. Though this does worry Shadow considerably. If the rumor is true and he's stronger during the day then this is clearly only a slight fraction of his true power, making Shadow all the more determined to end this without having to fight him. Yuki then waves his hand over the trio and a badge with a symbol of a peacock appears on the three's chests with various shades of purple.

"Because of the disrespect that one of you showed. You three will now each face a challenge before you can even hope to even face me. I do apologize to the other two though, but my challenges need at least three devils to have them fully tested and this just seems like a perfect chance to do that," says Yuki as he points to his base.

Silt looks at Yuki like he should fight him right now. Lina on the other hand keeps staring at the base. Shadow just drops his head, sighs, and starts walking to the base. Lina sees Shadow walking, then grabs Silt and starts following him. Silt, confused, just accepts this and goes with the others while trying to keep his eyes focused on Yuki. While the three of them start walking to the base, Yuki teleports back into his base to wait for them.

The Three Challenges

When they get to the base, Shadow notices that the base looks to be made of marble or at least something similar. They reach the base's main door and notice it's completely wooden with metal bands holding it together. The door is also almost twice the height of them and wide enough to fit all three of them at the same time. The entryway also seems far longer than it really should, but the three of them ignore it. They walk inside and see only an empty stone room with orbs, similar to what is used on the lanterns in the city, lighting the room. As the room is lighting up they notice that the room is made of solid stone blocks all the way around, ranging from rectangles to squares, all of various sizes, probably to form a pattern, but none of them really care. The stones are also made of a different material than the outside, most likely granite or limestone.

With the room completely lit they notice a sign in the middle of the room. The sign only says to wait for the challenges to begin. There doesn't seem to be any way out other than the door they came in. Unfortunately it's now fully closed and seemingly locked now. Even if it wasn't they knew they wouldn't get very far out.

Silt looks at Lina, still covering her face, with anger. "What was that for? I could've taken him right there! Hey wait, now that I have a better look you seem familiar!" yelled Silt.

"She did that because he already issued challenges, so he can't or won't face you till we complete them. Also, Lina, please take those bandanas off already," says Shadow in an exhausted tone, just done with the two of them.

Lina is surprised that Shadow knows it's her. "When did you figure it out?" asks Lina while she removes the bandanas covering her face.

"When I left the inn I knew you were following me. If I knew this was what you were going to do I would've said something earlier," says Shadow.

"Sorry, but I have a reason for it," apologizes Lina.

"Is one of those reasons avoiding me? Because it seems to be some-thing that you're good at. Don't even think that I've given up yet. I still want those answers, and now there's nowhere for you to run to," says Silt, getting right next to Lina.

He grabs Lina's arm to make sure she can't run away again. Lina becomes increasingly more nervous because she knows she can't avoid the situation. Silt starts asking her questions, which she responds to by trying to avoid the answer, which just gets on Silts nerves more. While they talk a magic circle appears near them. Shadow, who is just trying to not get involved in this whole conflict, sees it. He sighs and walks to the other two and breaks them up. Confused, Shadow just points to the magic circle that appeared.

"It seems that our challenges begin now," says Shadow.

"Alright, we can settle this later Lina, but for now let's do this," says Silt, getting hyped.

Hopefully I can get what I came here for while they are busy with their challenges, thinks Lina.

I just hope we can get through this without any more issues, thinks Shadow with increasing doubt.

As Silt tries to step onto the circle he runs into another invisible wall. "What the? What in hell is going on? Why can't I get on the damn circle?" says Silt in an irritated tone.

Shadow looks at the circle and then at the badges on each of them. "It's because that's not your challenge Silt, it's mine. It matches the color of my badge," says Shadow, pointing at his badge.

Silt realizes what Shadow is saying and looks at their badges. He then steps away from the portal so Shadow can step up. Shadow steps into the portal with no issue and gets teleported away.

Shadow teleports into a new room that at first looks somewhat similar to where he just was. The only differences are a circular metallic pedestal with three animals resting atop it. The three animals are a lion, a horse, and a peacock. He also notices that upon a closer inspection the walls are also different. Unlike the last room the floor, wall, and ceiling seem to be made of evenly sized cube stones.

OK, so what exactly do I do here? thinks Shadow.

Immediately after thinking that, the badge on Shadow pulls itself from his body and heads to the pedestal and merges with it. After that the pedestal's color turns into the same color as the badge that was just on Shadow. After that a screen appears in the first room where Silt and Lina were. It seems that its purpose is so that they can see Shadow's challenge. The pedestal begins to sink into the ground as some of the stone cubes start moving away, causing a pathway to open. Behind the door stands a statue of a woman. The statue is made of some kind of gray stone.

"Huh?" says Shadow, tilting his head, confused at what's going on.

The statue starts moving and draws two stone axes. As it does the statue starts changing different colors. Within a few seconds the statue is fully colored and now resembles a living being then a statue.

"Defeat the guardian," says a voice in Shadow's head out of nowhere.

Huh, what was that? thinks Shadow, becoming more confused at what is going on.

As soon as it was said the statue erupts with a giant aura. This confuses Shadow even more and the statue begins charging at him. As the statue gets closer Shadow re-centers himself and draws his sword. Seeing him draw his sword the statue then starts charging toward Shadow. However he doesn't move from his original spot. As it gets closer Shadow prepares to attack.

"What is he doing? He's just standing there. He seemed more proactive with the dragons," says Silt, confused, seeing what Shadow's doing.

"Just wait, I'm sure he knows what he's doing. You already saw just how strong he is, so something like this will be nothing for him," responds Lina.

Then, as the statue gets right next to Shadow, he disappears. He then appears a few steps behind the statue and begins to sheath his sword. As he does the statue then breaks in half starting at the tip of the head, showing where Shadow cut it. The two halves both hit the floor at the same time while emitting a loud thud. With the statue fully collapsed it melds into the floor, almost like if it were made of clay, and as it does the pedestal reemerges from the floor along with the magic circle. The screen in the first room also disappears. Shadow also sees that the horse on top of the pedestal is now the color his badge was while the rest of the pedestal has returned to its original color. Shadow notices this and comes up with the theory that it could just mean that his challenge is complete, but can't say for certain.

Something doesn't seem right about that fight to me. It seemed far too easy. Why? Could it be because it was to test it like he said? Hmm, I wonder if it could also be something like that? Well for now I guess I'll have to wait and observe the other challenges to see if my theory is right. While I'm at it I can see if my theory about what the pedestal is for is also correct, thinks Shadow as he starts walking to the circle.

Shadow walks into the circle and is teleported back to the original room with Lina and Silt. Both are happy to see how well he did. Both however are not aware that he feels that something was off about the challenge. The two feel a wave of confidence and slight arrogance upon seeing how easy Shadow had it.

"HAHAHA that was great, you sure went through that challenge like it was nothing," says Silt.

"He's right, Shadow, that was great, we're one step closer," says Lina.

Well I mean if I couldn't even do that much I wouldn't be able to make it very far on this journey. Though that still doesn't change the fact that that challenge felt way easier than it should have. Should I tell them what I think is going on? No, I probably shouldn't for now. If I do and I'm right it might diminish their confidence. On the other hand if I tell them and I'm wrong then they would worry for nothing and be furious with me. For now it might be best to just stay quiet, thinks Shadow as he nods his head with a worried expression hidden under his mask.

The circle in the room changes to a different shade of purple, matching the color of the badge on Lina.

"Well, then I guess it's my turn," says Lina while looking at the circle.

While I'm in there I can check to see if there's a secret passage that can lead me right to Yuki, thinks Lina.

As Lina steps just outside of the circle for her challenge Shadow suddenly notices something is now different about the room. It's another magic circle. This one however is a more pure purple color along with a different pattern on it than the one that Lina was about to step on. *Huh, this wasn't here earlier. Why did it appear? Did it appear because I had finished my challenge? Why aren't the other two not responding to it? Do they not see it? Should I speak up about it? Then again I don't know what that one will lead to. If the others can't see it it might be good to not worry them about it. Plus if they know about it they might just jump in without completing their challenges. I think for now I should just keep quiet about this as well until one of them says something,* thinks Shadow.

Lina secretly and briefly looks at Shadow without him knowing. From what she sees she notices that he's looking at something that doesn't appear to be there. Immediately she comes to a conclusion as if she knows what's going on. *Hmph, so that's his method for challenges. I guess it's better than the previous one's method of only letting those she liked to pass regardless if they completed their challenge or not. So if I can't find a passage I'll just take the path that Shadow sees to head to Yuki. It's a win-win either way,* thinks Lina.

Lina steps into the first circle and gets teleported to the same room Shadow was just in. She quickly notices the pedestal and notices that one of the three animals is a different color from both the others and the pedestal itself. She comes to the same conclusion that Shadow did about it, but this time is certain of it. She also quickly looks around the room and sees that there's currently no way in or out which leaves her a bit distraught.

Damn, there doesn't really seem to be a way out after all. In the end I guess I have no choice but to complete this challenge to get where I need to, thinks Lina.

Lina's badge floats over to the pedestal. It changes to the color of her badge except for the horse and goes down just as it did before. The screen in the first room reappears and Shadow looks somewhat confused.

"Did this happen during my challenge?" asks Shadow.

"Yeah, let's see if she can get through her challenge as easily as you did. I'm actually curious what she'll fight. Will it be the same or different from what you faced? Either way I'm curious to see how she fights when putting real effort into it. Though she's strong she also seems to be the type who runs away when at all possible. Though she can't really run away this time," rambles Silt, with Shadow drowning out most of it.

Hm, now let's see if I'm right about my theory. Also, that thing's still bugging me, thinks Shadow as he momentarily looks away from the screen.

When the pedestal leaves the room the top three rows of the walls start moving, leaving an opening around the ceiling.

"Survive and defeat the horde," says the mysterious voice in Lina's head.

Right after that, purple imps start emerging from the opening and start filling the room. When they finish coming out of the opening the count is one hundred purple imps, all armed with pure Pride energy spears, which are stronger than the pitchforks the group from earlier used.

Yep, that figures. I can't tell if this was done intentionally or is just a coincidence. Either way it's both ironic and annoying. Well this does give me a chance to try out what Shadow apparently did, thinks Lina in both an annoyed and slight upbeat tone.

"Well this doesn't look good for her. What do you think about this, Shadow? Do you think she'll be ok?" asks Silt, seeing Lina's situation.

Shadow nods, looking back at the screen showing Lina. The imps start swarming Lina, but she shows signs that she will be fine this time around. Shadow notices that she is using the fighting method that he told her about earlier. Even with one hundred imps swarming her she handles them with relative ease. turning it from one versus one hundred to one-on-one one hundred times. In a few minutes she finishes off the last of the imps with little difficulty. Silt is stunned by Lina's feat while Shadow is only slightly surprised, not that she handled them, but that she understood and implemented his method that he learned from Eve so quickly. Now finished, the pedestal returns and the magic circle reappears. Now the lion, just like the horse, is the only part that retains the color of her badge. Lina notices this and walks into the circle without giving it much thought.

As Lina comes back to the first room Shadow and Silt look over at her. Shadow seems to still be staring off into space while thinking about something as Silt looks toward Lina.

"That was amazing, you handled those imps like they were nothing. I knew you were strong, but taking on a hoard of imps with such ease... That technique that you used was really something too. I never would have thought to fight the swarm one at a time," says Silt in an excited tone.

"Thanks, fighting them was child's play. Shadow's method really did seem to work out in the end. Though it did get a little tedious after a while," responds Lina arrogantly while she looks over at Shadow while he stands by himself, still in thought. *Still, you can't argue with the results after all. Maybe I should try it on other swarms too. Though then again I doubt that method would work on most demon hordes. Either way, thank you Shadow for telling me about this method*, thinks Lina.

Shadow snaps out of thought since he heard Lina talking about him. All he really heard is her being a bit condescending about his technique and calling it tedious. He looks over to the two of them. "Sorry about that, but I'm glad it came in handy for you," says Shadow in a slightly sad tone.

Lina can tell that Shadow seems a bit more depressed than he was before she went in and wonders why. She quickly realizes it's because she worded what she said about his technique wrong, as well as her not saying the praise to Shadow out loud. *Ah fuck, it just sounded like I was mocking him and by extension Eve. I need to clear this up fast or this is going to get really awkward during Silt's challenge. Should I say something now or when Silt leaves? I should probably do it now. If I wait it'll probably just make things even more awkward*, thinks Lina, panicking internally. "Uh, Shadow," says Lina.

Though before she can say more Silt speaks up about what she said. "So you just used his method and it worked, but after you're finished using it you start acting arrogant about how easy it is, as well as complaining to him about using it, REALLY?! Jeez, I can't believe that you are someone that is so ungrateful. You could at least thank him for teaching you it. Also if it's so tedious then why in hell did you use it!? It's those like you that steal and use others' techniques and pass them off as their own and/or mock the technique altogether that I despise more than anything in all of hell," says Silt, irritated by Lina's attitude. Silt then just stares at Lina with anger in his eyes.

Lina quickly looks away from both of them from embarrassment and a bit of shame from being called out. Mostly because she knows that Silt has a point. She also hates devils and monsters like that, which makes her feel like a hypocrite. Shadow looks at Silt, who is still angry at Lina.

"Just one more to go and it's your turn Silt," says Shadow, wanting to change the subject.

Silt looks away from Lina and back at the circle. He starts calming down from his rant and starts getting hyped for his challenge. "All right, it's finally my turn, let's go!" says Silt, excited to finally have his turn.

As Silt steps through the circle Lina looks back in their direction and sees something new has appeared in the room. "Huh, what's that doing here now?" asks Lina.

Just as before, Silt appears in the challenge room and his badge goes into the pedestal. The screen reappears in the first room again, though only Shadow is watching it. A section of the wall farthest from him sinks back. What replaces it is a button switch now on the other side of the room. The floor also starts moving and most of the squares start descending, leaving Silt on a small platform on the opposite wall of the switch with other platforms leading to it.

"Make your way to the end and push the switch—" says the mysterious voice.

The voice is about to say something else, but Silt doesn't wait. "Huh, seems easy enough," says Silt as he jumps to the closest platform.

As soon as he touches the platform, part of the ceiling comes down and collides with the platform Silt is on, seemingly squashing him.

"—while avoiding the blocks from the ceiling trying to squash you," continues the mysterious voice.

Geez, is it even possible to even pass that challenge? I guess that definitely proves my theory, but jeez that seems like overkill. Hey wait, what's that coming out? thinks Shadow.

Something looking like sand starts coming from where Silt was squashed. The sand then gathers together, then begins jumping from platform to platform while avoiding or being unaffected by the blocks coming down on it. The pile of sand finally makes its way to the switch. As it gets to the last platform the squares from the ceiling and other three walls start rushing toward it. The four blocks collide, but the sand just seeps through them. It then reaches and pushes the switch and the room goes back to normal. The sand heads back to Silt's clothes and starts forming into a shape and forms into Silt and he looks really mad.

So he's some kind of sand-based monster, hm. Well either way, he doesn't look happy, though I can't blame him, thinks Shadow.

The pedestal returns with the last animal adopting the color of his badge. The magic circle reappears on the other end of the room where Silt started. The pedestal starts spinning with the three shades of purple radiating from the pedestal. Silt braces himself and starts running for the circle, thinking that it might explode. He runs straight toward the circle while swerving around the pedestal. Unfortunately he only makes it halfway and is basically next to the pedestal when it stops and the purple shades start condensing at the heads of the animals. Shadow sees this on the screen and becomes more and more nervous about the situation. He wants to warn Silt, but knows that it would be pointless. Silt however does see this and tries to run even faster, but then hears a pop. Against his better judgment he looks behind him and sees what looks like purple confetti. Both Silt and Shadow are confused. "What?" the two of them say in very confused voices.

Silt goes from being irritated to furious. Shadow can even see his eye starting to twitch before the screen disappears. A loud scream can be heard coming from above him. Shadow can tell that it's Silt and can understand why he's screaming. Once finished with his rage-filled scream Silt walks onto the circle and reappears in the first room. He only sees Shadow as he walks up to him to vent.

"WHAT IN HELL WAS THAT?!! That was BULLSHIT! If I wasn't a sand golem I'd be dead. Why was mine more difficult, HUH? ALSO, WHAT THE FUCK was with that pedestal at the end? Also, WHERE THE FUCK is Lina? Did she run away again?" asks Silt, looking at Shadow, obviously angry with what happened.

Huh, so he's a golem and not a devil. Huh, well, I didn't ask and I just assumed. So that's what a golem looks like. Uh-oh, looks like he's getting angrier by the second. I better tell him what I know before he goes on a rampage, thinks Shadow, looking over to Silt.

"Ok, I think I know what happened, but first I'm going to need you to please take a deep breath and calm down," says Shadow while giving a calm-down gesture to Silt.

Silt takes Shadow's advice and starts to take some deep breaths. He starts feeling some guilt for screaming at him. He's the only one here that he's not actually mad at. Finally back in a calm state he looks at Shadow. "Ok, I'm calm now, and sorry for screaming at you. I just really needed to vent my frustration. So anyways, you said that you know what's going on," says Silt while he rubs the right side of his neck with his left hand.

Shadow nods toward Silt, showing that he understands and confirming his question. "First off, don't worry about it. I understand that you needed to vent out your anger with what happened. It's not the first time I've been used as a front for someone to take out their anger on so I'm used to it," says Shadow.

"Though those times were more physical than oral," whispers Shadow.

"Huh," says Silt.

"Nothing. Anyways, counting your challenge, I can say my theory is correct. The shade of purple badges did represent the difficulty of our challenges. Since I praised Pride I was given an easier challenge, and since you tripped him you got a far harder if not near impossible challenge," responds Shadow, trying to keep Silt calm about the situation.

"Hmph, and Lina did nothing so she got an intermediate-level challenge, huh? Also, where did she go?" asks Silt, looking around and seeing that it really is just the two of them in the room.

Shadow points to a second magic circle separate from the one they are currently using. "She left here already," says Shadow.

"What the…? How long has that been there?" asks Silt, confused by the second circle.

"I saw it after I finished my challenge so Lina probably did too after hers. My guess is it becomes visible and usable when someone finishes their challenge. She stepped onto it right after you left. I however chose to stay and watch your challenge. It wouldn't have been fair to you to not watch you take on your challenge when you did for me," says Shadow.

"Well that was rude of her. You on the other hand are a good man. I was curious what kind of devil, monster, or reaper you were. Now I can say for sure that you are a respectable devil and I'm glad to have met you. Well then, should we get going then, and give Pride a challenge of his own?" asks Silt, finally fully calmed down from everything and thinking more clearly.

Shadow smiles under his mask at what Silt said about him. Without saying a word he nods and the two of them walk into the second circle.

A Prideful Fight

The two appear in what appears like a large dining hall. The room has an elegant feel to it and is decorated as such. Everything looks to be high quality, from the decorations to even the walls and floor that make up the room. While looking around, Shadow also notices that the material used for the room is just like what is used for the outside of the base. It is completely different from the previous two rooms. Shadow becomes uneasy because he isn't sure if they are safer or not by being here.

They then notice a long dining table completely full of food. There they see Pride eating with two attendants on each side. The two are a man and a woman both wearing nice suits and each wearing the mask of an animal. The mask on the man is a fox and the mask on the woman is a rabbit. Silt quickly recognizes them as the masked devils that stole the dragon corpses earlier. Also already sitting at the table is Lina with a sad look on her face.

"Have a seat, I will deal with you after I've finished this meal," says Yuki as he continues to eat.

Shadow and Silt both walk over and take a seat at the table. After sitting down Shadow notices something about Yuki that he didn't see outside. Yuki's eyes are a dull purple, as though they are still changing from their original color.

As Shadow sat down he got a closer look at the food. There is a large variety of meat-based dishes. He can tell that all of these meat dishes on the table are made from the dragons that Shadow killed earlier. There are also multiple plates of vegetables and fruits, and bowls of several types of breads. There is also a life-size ice sculpture of a peacock, possibly for either show or to help keep some food cool. He even notices that the tablecloth is of very high quality, a pure shade of purple, and the edges are adorn with a pattern of lions and horses. Unsure of what to do he keeps his hands in his lap and waits for something to be said.

"Oh, did you have all of this prepared for us completing your stupid challenges?" asks Silt as he sits down.

"No you rude ignorant golem! I was eating when you invaded my home. Also my challenges aren't stupid. Honestly I was showing you what happens when you mess with a sin," responds Yuki while still eating.

"We're sorry for interrupting your meal, it was completely unintentional. Were you expecting guests with all the food here?" asks Shadow, still feeling uneasy while gesturing at all the food.

"No, we sins use a lot of energy to give energy to protect our territories and contain the excess energy from the sinners. That's especially needed now since some of us have a heavy load of sinners right now. So that's why we sins need to eat large amounts of food as a result," says Yuki, who stopped eating momentarily to answer Shadow.

While Yuki continues to eat, Shadow happens to see something off in another room from an open door. Through the door there are gems like the ones used in the city to keep it safe.

Hm, he must be remaking new gems to bring back the towns that were destroyed. He must really want to be ready to bring this territory back to normal, thinks Shadow.

Within a matter of minutes the huge spread of food is eaten up. Yuki picks up his glass chalice and begins slightly swirling the wine inside around. "You know I was actually quite impressed by your abilities during your challenge. You took her out with only one slash. It even gave me a bit of joy watching you destroy her. Granted that copy was only about one tenth of the real one's power, but it was still an incredible feat," says Yuki while staring into his chalice.

"The real one?" asks Shadow

"Well years ago before I became a sin I was part of a small team of three like yours here. We were strong, or at least we believed we were strong enough to take on one of the guardians left over from armageddon. Let's just say that we got hit with reality hard, but I did win eventually. That victory in fact was what got me scouted out to become the new sin of pride," says Yuki.

"If you don't mind me asking, could you tell me what happened during your fight with the guardian?" asks Shadow.

Yuki thinks it over for a few seconds and then shrugs. "Aw why not, I mean you three are the first to complete my challenges. Plus I've really been wanting to tell others this story. So I guess I'll humor you and give you an abridged version of that time," says Yuki.

Shadow bows the best he can while sitting down in appreciation. "Thank you Lord Pride," says Shadow.

"Well to put it simply, myself and my two teammates found a guardian in a large crater. One of my teammates, who I will refer to as

Dew, said we should challenge it. Before me and our other teammate, who I'll call Bo, could answer he jumped down. Since we couldn't just leave him to die we jumped down after him. The guardian looked like a woman brandishing two axes. She was also very strong and even three on one didn't faze her. We brandished our weapons of a war hammer for me, a great axe for Bo, and a broadsword for Dew and just went right at her. Though something was a bit strange because even though all three of us attacked her she had some weird hatred focused on Dew. She did attack us from time to time near the beginning, but she mostly focused on Dew first. Because of that he got more pissed from getting constantly attacked even if he was the farthest one away from her while myself and Bo laughed about it while still trying to fight her while he tried to patch up his injuries. After some time Bo summoned up some demonic cats that he'd tamed. At first they attacked the guardian, but then while we weren't looking at him, for some reason, Dew started acting crazy, well crazier than he usually is, and started saying gibberish while moving his sword like a wand. I could hear some of it though I had no idea what he was saying, but it seemed like the demonic cats could. They suddenly started attacking him instead, and within a matter of moments Dew died. Myself, Bo, and even the guardian just stood there wondering what the fuck just happened. However while she was distracted I took a small knife I had in my pocket and stabbed the guardian in the chest several times. It seemed that doing that gave me one of her skills. Seeing the guardian in pain Bo also started attacking her again. The fight continued for a few days. The guardian was near death, but so were Bo and I. Just before I finished off the guardian Bo fell over dead from all of his injuries. Pissed, I grabbed Dew's sword and Bo's axe to pin her legs, and then her own axes to pin her arms. I raised my hammer and brought it down onto her head. It was silent after that, then a light shined from her and went into me, then went back to silence. After that I passed out and the next thing I knew I was surrounded by six of the sins. They praised my and my team's accomplishment. Though it was a bittersweet victory I thanked them for the praise. Sloth then offered me the opportunity to become a sin and replace the one that was causing a lot of trouble. With no better option I took the offer. When I fought her to take her position it was laughable how weak she was compared to the guardian. You all should probably know the rest after that. Wow that really feels like a weight was taken off my shoulders. Though I guess it wasn't very abridged now was it, huh," says Yuki, shrugging his shoulders as he finishes his story.

Shadow notices that Yuki seemed somewhat both sad and happy retelling this story. Seeing this he believes that Yuki isn't making it up to garner sympathy. Though this doesn't change his mind that he still came for his key. He bows to Yuki again. "No, I appreciate you telling us such a story. I'm sorry for your loss. Though I do wonder what made your friend act so crazy before he died," says Shadow, lifting his head.

"So do I. My guess is that he just snapped from being mostly singled out before he died. Though thinking back on it now I did notice a strange cloud that was passing past the crater. Maybe that had something to do with it?" says Yuki, who suddenly looks at Lina.

Lina turns her head to avoid eye contact.

"I think I know what you're talking about. I think a similar cloud engulfed me earlier today. Though it didn't drive me mad like your teammate. All it did was show me visions, but maybe if I stayed in it longer it could have driven me mad," says Shadow.

Lina remains silent and starts nervously sweating. Before Yuki can say anything about what Shadow said, Silt, whose patience has run out, slams down on the table and stands up. "That's enough! I came here for a fight, not to watch you stuff your face and talk about the past!" says Silt as he jumps forward and throws a punch at Yuki.

Before the punch can even make contact it is completely blocked by the female attendant with little effort. Silt becomes more irritated that his punch was blocked again and by the same masked devil from before. Yuki gives an exhausted sigh at Silt's rude behavior. He then stands and Shadow sees what he went on his journey for.

A key.

A large purple key is attached to his belt, one that he didn't have when he met them outside.

"Fine, I'll just humor you and show you the difference between the two of us," says Yuki, just done dealing with Silt. Yuki snaps his fingers and circles form around all four of them. The two attendants are about to also step into the circle, but they wait when Yuki gestures to them to stay back.

The four of them appear on the top of the base. The top is a flat stone platform made of the same material as all the other rooms they were in. At the edge of the platform they're on there seems to be a chasm separating the edge of the platform and the wall of the roof. Just above them is the top of the giant tree seen from the entrance, hovering over them. Lights around the edge of the base start to turn on to illuminate the area.

Yuki looks over to Shadow and Lina. He begins apologizing for bringing the two of them here as well. "I apologize for bringing you two along with us. You were just within the area of my teleportation skill. Just go over to the side so you don't get involved. I'll take you out of the barrier once I'm finished with this disrespectful moron," says Yuki.

Lina starts walking to the side of the platform without saying a word. Shadow still sees the key attached to Yuki and thinks he can use this to his advantage. "Oh great Lord Pride, before you fight this man, may I please ask you for a favor?" asks Shadow.

"Hm, well since you are so respectful and I do owe you for handling those dragons, I'll hear you out. What is this favor that you wish to ask, bo... er, Shadow?" asks Yuki while looking down his nose at Shadow.

"May I please borrow that key that you have there for a while sir?" asks Shadow.

Yuki looks at the key on his belt, then looks at Shadow with a now angered look. "So that's what you were after all this time. It was foolish of me to think you were a respectable fighter and loyal follower. I was warned someone like you would come sooner or later. I'll kill you where you stand, you heretic," says Yuki, getting more enraged at Shadow.

Huh, heretic. Well whatever happens, it's clear that he won't give me the key. It also doesn't seem like escape is an option now either. Well I guess I have no choice now I guess. I hope I don't screw this up, thinks Shadow.

Yuki's aura starts increasing. It grows outward from his body, then retracts. His aura now hugs his body with a deep purple covering him. Shadow charges at him while drawing his sword and strikes Yuki. Shadow is able to inflict a shallow cut from the chest to the stomach.

Yuki dodges his attack just in time to avoid worse damage. "Figures you would pull a move like that, heretic," says Yuki.

Silt runs over to Shadow, irritated. "Hey, this is my fight, stay out of this," says Silt.

"I need that key that he has, and he's not giving me any other choice. How about we work together to fight him?" responds Shadow.

"Why, beating him shouldn't be that difficult. Besides, it seems like it should be easier because he isn't using that power he used on the bridge!" exclaims Silt.

"No, he is, it's just condensed so it will act like armor for him. My sword was just barely able to get past it before he moved out of the way. He won't be easy to fight if either of us tries to take him alone," answers Shadow.

Silt already can tell that what Shadow is saying is the truth, but he doesn't want to admit it out loud. Silt sighs. "Fine, but just don't get in my way. Also, don't blame me if you get hurt, you got that Shadow?" says Silt.

Shadow nods and the two of them charge towards to Yuki.

Shadow and Silt start double-teaming Yuki and making sure that he doesn't have a chance to fight back much. Shadow fights him up close with his sword, cutting through his concentrated prideful aura. Silt stays at a distance to strike him with his sand to push him back. When he gets a chance Silt gets close and strikes Yuki with his sand-like fists.

For some reason Yuki doesn't even try too hard to fight them both back, though Yuki does fight back a little. He blasts a bullet of his aura at Silt and Shadow and pushes them back to the edge to the platform.

Both of them look down and are surprised by what they see.

"Fuck that was close, I can't even see what's down there, can you Shadow?" asks Silt.

Shadow can in fact see down all the way to the bottom of the pit thanks to his new eyes. All he can see at the bottom are spikes lining the walls and floor of the chasm.

"It's better that you don't know. As long as we stay out of it then it won't be an issue," answers Shadow.

Silt nods at Shadow and the two of them charge back at Yuki to continue fighting him while trying to get his key. With each strike against him, Yuki seems to hurt more and more.

Wait, this seems far too easy, why isn't he even trying to fight back against us? Wait, he's not fighting us back on purpose, thinks Shadow, realizing what is happening.

Shadow stops fighting, leaving Silt to keep attacking. With one last hit Silt causes Yuki to fall.

"Ha, that was easier than I thought. Hey, why did you stop fighting?" asks Silt as he points to Shadow.

It's clear to Shadow that Silt is starting to get exhausted from the fight. He can tell Silt wouldn't have won if the fight lasted much longer.

As he thinks that, a loud laughter can be heard. Silt wonders where the laughter is coming from.

It turns out that the laughter is coming from Yuki as he rises back up like nothing happened. "You thought that you could really defeat me? It's clear that one of you isn't a complete fool since you eventually realized my strategy," says Yuki while looking at Shadow.

Shadow looks over at Silt and sees that he's both surprised and a bit depressed that all his effort was all for nothing. "So everything I did was for nothing," whispers Silt to himself, but he's overheard by Shadow. Silt tilts his head down and starts trembling slightly out of anger and sadness.

Shadow walks over to Silt to console him. "Listen, right now, defeating him seems like it isn't a viable action. So let's just grab his key and get out of here while we still can. I have a plan that might let us win so listen up," whispers Shadow.

Silt doesn't respond and falls to his knees, ready to accept defeat. It seems he heard what Shadow said, but he doesn't respond, believing it is pointless. With Silt on the ground and Lina off to the side, Shadow stands alone to fight Yuki.

"And then there was one, the heretic. You know, it's fitting I fight you up here. Here my predecessor can watch and see how a real sin handles a problem," says Yuki, pointing and looking at the giant tree.

"Wait, so then that giant tree really is—" asks Shadow before getting interrupted.

"Yep, that's her, or at the very least her sin tree. Since she was the former and original sin of pride it should be no surprise. A fitting punishment for her really," says Yuki.

Yuki suddenly jumps up to the tree and tears off a leaf. A very faint scream can be heard below them. As he lands he shows the leaf, which is flowing with a strong aura, and bites it. The aura immediately disappears from the leaf. Shadow notices that Yuki's power is increasing and his aura armor is becoming more dense.

So he can absorb energy from the leaves of these trees. Why show this now when he already has the advantage? I guess he just wants to make it clear about the difference in strength he has over us, thinks Shadow.

"So do you want to keep fighting a pointless battle, or do you just want to take the easy way out like your companions and surrender?" asks Yuki.

Shadow faces Yuki with his sword in hand. *I don't need to defeat him. I just need to grab his key and run, then find a way past the barrier around here. Sounds simple enough. Here's hoping I don't fuck it up though and die*, thinks Shadow.

Shadow charges toward Yuki, who just brushes him off and sends him flying to the edge of the platform. Shadow can see just over the platform and sees all the spikes lining the walls and floor of the drop-off point between the platform and wall. Yuki moves over to him and grabs him by his neck and holds him over the pit. While holding Shadow over the pit Yuki is strangling him with one hand.

"A fitting end for you, heretic, to fall at my hands. It's too bad I won't be able to watch you being impaled, but hearing your screams makes a fair compromise. Now die while knowing you will never be better than me or most of the sins!" exclaims Yuki.

With that, he drops Shadow into the spiked pit.

One Down, Six to Go

Lina looks over in great shock, watching Shadow fall.

Silt just looks over at Yuki while still on his knees.

Yuki looks back at Silt with a smug smile. "Now that the heretic has been dealt with, I can take care of you, you arrogant monster," says Yuki while looking down his nose at Silt.

Silt looks at Yuki with anger, sadness, and fear. Silt then starts looking just above Yuki and starts to smile.

Lina also looks over Yuki and also starts smiling herself.

Yuki is confused why the both of them are smiling and starts getting annoyed by it. "Why in hell are the two of you smiling?" asks Yuki, noticing they are looking above him.

Yuki turns around and looks up and sees Shadow floating above them. Seeing him still alive enrages Yuki even more.

Thankfully that skill scroll I got from the shop was levitation, thinks Shadow.

Shadow then begins to charge Yuki from the air.

"In the air or on the ground, the result will still be the same!" exclaims Yuki, preparing to intercept Shadow's attack.

Shadow clashes with Yuki, which actually causes a deeper cut than he caused before, though he sees it isn't going to make much difference with Yuki's aura still protecting him. Shadow floats back up to try and stay out of range.

"HAHAHA, is that all you can do now, heretic?! I guess I should just stop toying with you and just take you out!" exclaims Yuki as he puts his hand over his pendant. His pendant glows and he pulls out a sword. The sword is different from Shadow's because for some reason the hilt looks like it's half hammer and half axe.

Fuck, this doesn't look good. I might not be able to finish this easily or at all, thinks Shadow, looking at Yuki's weapon.

"Don't you see the difference? You are just a heretic, and I AM A GOOOOOD! AH!" exclaims Yuki while getting hit from behind. Yuki turns around and sees Silt using sand to attack him when his back was turned. Silt has a smug look on his face. He's clearly pleased that he took advantage of Yuki's ego again. Pissed at Silt, Yuki starts going toward him, but with his back turned Shadow then attacks him and causes more damage to Yuki. Then when Yuki turns back to Shadow, Silt attacks him again.

Shadow and Silt continue this strategy and make some headway, but they still aren't able to get the key from Yuki. Shadow and Silt become more and more exhausted as this goes on.

Crap, we aren't getting much further than we were earlier. Plus with that ability he'll just heal himself, thus making our efforts all for nothing. We need to grab his key and get out of here fast, thinks Shadow.

Yuki is becoming more enraged the longer the fight continues and has finally reached his limit. "That's it, I'm done dealing with you fools!" exclaims Yuki while turning toward Silt. Yuki charges toward Silt, seeing him as the easier target to take out first.

Seeing this, Silt tries to defend himself, but Yuki is able to break through and start attacking Silt with his weapon. Being exhausted from attacking Yuki earlier, Silt is only able to do very little to defend against Yuki's attacks. Silt just keeps getting hurt and eventually just falls down in defeat, barely able to move.

"Now that he's finished I can take care of you, heretic, once and for all! I will make sure you pathetic fools learn your place permanently!" exclaims Yuki.

After seeing Yuki defeat Silt, Shadow grips his sword in anger at both Yuki and himself for being so weak. *Damn it, I hate people like him! Thinking he's superior to others just because he has more power and authority. He sees us as insects. If we can just get past his aura and grab his damn key, we won't have to deal with him anymore!* thinks Shadow. *Let's just end him. Take him out and take the key,* thinks Shadow.

Fueled by this, Shadow charges toward Yuki with greater force than before. "Ha, it's pointless, you heretic. Try all you want, the results will be the same," says Yuki, ready to stop Shadow's attack.

Just before reaching Yuki, Shadow's sword starts producing a dark shadowlike aura. He slashes at Yuki, which cuts right through his aura armor and causes a deep cut to Yuki. From what the two of them saw, it almost seems like this new strange dark aura absorbed the aura covering Yuki before cutting him.

Realizing what just happened, Yuki backs away quickly. "WHAT IN HELL JUST HAPPENED?!" exclaims Yuki, confused by what just happened. Yuki looks even more confused because now his aura won't cover the entire area.

Shadow begins to charge again, with Yuki preparing to retaliate.

I won't let him get another lucky shot. Huh? thinks Yuki when he sees something rolling toward him.

Lina rolls some balls over by Yuki, and as they reach him, smoke starts coming from them. Shadow stops his charge after seeing the smoke. Within a matter of seconds Yuki is surrounded by a fog of smoke and can barely see around him. Yuki becomes enraged by what Lina has done.

"WHY LINA WOULD YOU SIDE WITH THIS HERETIC?! YOU GOOD-FOR-NOTHING TRAITOR!" yells Yuki.

With Yuki distracted Shadow continues his charge and gets right next to Yuki. He tries to reach for the key, but Yuki notices him and begins to swing his weapon. Shadow notices this and avoids it and retaliates with his own attack. From Shadow's point of view, Yuki's movements seem slower than before. With this, Shadow is able to land a direct blow across Yuki's torso while continuing to cut through his aura with ease. This slash is so severe that Yuki is sent flying outside of the smoke cloud and lands on his back. A slight cracking sound can be heard, but no one pays attention to it. Lina and Silt see this and are surprised. Shadow returns to the ground and walks out of the smoke toward Yuki.

With Yuki still on his back, Shadow reaches down and takes the key. Yuki can do little about it because even though he is healing it is slowed down. He realizes this is due to the strange aura that Shadow has around his sword. Knowing he's been beaten, he just looks straight at Shadow.

"Well what are you waiting for, you want to finish me off, don't you? That's the goal of a heretic like you. Just know the other sins will come after you," says Yuki.

Do it, take that sword and end him. It's the only way to win. They deserve what they get, thinks Shadow. "No, I already have the key, so there's no reason to end you. My goal is to get back my friend that you sins kidnapped. So if that makes me a heretic in your eyes then so be it," says Shadow as he puts the key away.

The shadowlike aura disappears and Shadow sheaths his sword.

Yuki looks at Shadow in surprise. "Wait what!?" says Yuki, realizing that he made a mistake.

Shadow ignores Yuki and he and Lina both walk over to Silt. Shadow helps him up to his feet. Shadow then gets a good grip on both Silt and Lina, then starts levitating. The three of them start heading to the entrance of the base.

Yuki, still lying on the floor, looks over at the giant pride tree of the previous Pride while his two attendants arrive to give him medical aid. *So he wasn't a heretic. He was just someone trying to save his friend. To think that a human would actually come all the way to hell for his friend. It's been so long that I almost forgot what it means to have true friendship with someone and what you would do for them. I was completely wrong about him both as a fighter and as a person. If I make a mistake that bad and still lose, how good of a sin will I be going forward? Will... will I just turn out just like her? No, I won't let that happen. I have too much pride as a sin and as the ruler of this territory to ever let that happen. To make sure of that I'll do what she never did and change myself,* thinks Yuki.

Shadow, Lina, and Silt stand at the entrance looking for a way past the forcefield holding them in.

"So how do we get past this thing?" asks Shadow.

"Why don't you try using that weird power you used against Pride?" responds Silt, still being helped by Shadow to stand.

"I'm not even sure how I did it in the first place or how to summon it again," says Shadow. *Also, those thoughts I had, what was with them? They were so angry. Was that what I really felt at the time? Is that what summoned that power?* thinks Shadow.

Seeing that Shadow is racking his brain about the whole situation, Lina starts to reach for her bag to grab something. As she does, the three of them can hear someone coming to them amongst all the screaming.

They turn around and see that it is Yuki who seems to have already recovered enough to be up and walking again, though barely. His two attendants are with him again, ready to grab him if he falls over. The three of them begin to worry, thinking he wants to continue the fight and take back the key.

Yuki then takes one hand and grabs his pendant and raises the other toward them. "Doorway open," says Yuki.

The force field then begins to open a hole for them to walk out of. The three of them see the hole, then look back at Yuki in confusion before Lina and Silt turn back around and start walking out, with Shadow not taking his eyes off Yuki.

With the other two out, Yuki snaps his fingers and the two attendants quickly disappear and reappear to his side, each now carrying a wooden box. Yuki grabs a hand-sized bag from one of the boxes and tosses it to Shadow. "That's your compensation for taking care of those dragons. I was planning to give you it in a more civilized way, but I guess that's no longer an option," says Yuki.

Shadow just nods his head. "Thank you for this," says Shadow.

Yuki now grabs the other items from the boxes his attendants are holding and tosses them to Shadow.

Shadow catches them and sees that they're a glass bottle with a red liquid and for some reason a crown.

"Think of these as an apology for our misunderstanding. That's an intermediate-level healing elixir. You can use that on the monster, not that the ungrateful bastard deserves it. I mistook you for someone else. If you really are here to save your friend, know that we took them for a reason," says Yuki.

"What reason could you have had for kidnapping my friend?" asks Shadow while Silt and Lina start walking through the hole.

"I'm sorry, but I can't tell you why we did that at this point in time, even if I fully knew why we did it in the first place. We were ordered by the leader of all the sins to stay quiet. Though I can tell you we never meant any ill intent for your friend. Right now she has them contained to keep them safe until the threat targeting them is gone," answers Yuki.

Shadow gives a long sigh, then starts walking to the hole, but Yuki calls him to tell him a few more things. "I have three more things to tell you. First, if you still plan to go after those keys to unlock what your friend is contained in. I will contact the other sins and tell them about you so there won't be more misunderstandings, but you might still need to fight some of them either way. They might do this as a way for you to prove yourself to them, or just for fun. Second, each member of the sins has another key that you'll need: the crown of pride is mine. You'll need them to open Sloth's front door. She doesn't really like non-sin guests much and won't just open the door for you, even with my message. Finally, the reason for our misunderstanding was because that threat I told you about is also after your friend. So now that you are also looking for the keys they might come after you as well. I'm not sure what reason they want your friend for, but it's clear that they will even resort to violence. So just be careful out there since you will now have others come after you to get to your friend," says Yuki.

Shadow turns back around and starts walking toward the hole. "Wouldn't be the first time," responds Shadow as he walks through the hole.

While Shadow walks through the hole the female assistant moves next to Yuki and removes her mask. She holds the mask so that her face is still covered from Shadow's perspective. She whispers to Yuki about something, believing that Shadow can't hear her.

Shadow, however, can actually hear that they are being watched, though he already knew that.

After Shadow passes the force field Yuki closes the hole. *This was all that I could do without the other sins questioning my motive. Though who knows whether or not the others will even listen to what I have to say. It might just make it harder for them. I can tell you're interested in them for a different reason, aren't you Lust?* thinks Yuki, noticing a small hovering camera spying on everything that happened.

Though unbeknownst to all of them a certain birdlike demon is also spying on everything as well. It keeps its eyes on Shadow, ready to move to follow him.

After passing the force field Shadow sees Lina and Silt over by a nearby wall. Shadow walks over to Silt, who is laid next to the wall by Lina.

"Here, take this, it should help," says Shadow, handing Silt the elixir.

"Oh thanks, um what flavor is it?" asks Silt.

"Uh, I don't know. Does that matter? Also why would it have a flavor?" asks Shadow.

"Huh, you don't know about it? Well, a low elixir with flavor can help increase the healing effect. Though if the flavor isn't something the drinker likes then it won't help as much. Like is it grape flavored? Because I don't really like grapes," says Silt.

"Low elixir?" whispers Shadow, looking at the elixir. "Look, I don't know what flavor it is. For all I know it's bacon flavored, just drink it please," responds Shadow.

"Fine, fine," says Silt.

Though a little hesitant, Silt starts to try and grab the bottle. Lina, annoyed thinking that he's hesitating because he's being picky, walks up to the two of them and snatches the bottle from Shadow and shoves it into Silt's mouth. "Stop being picky and just shut up and drink the damned thing you stupid monster!" exclaims Lina, annoyed by their back and forth.

Silt drinks it and is able to get up, not fully healed, but enough to walk around with no issues. Silt is irritated at Lina for what she did. "Damn it Lina, what in hell was that? I would have taken it without your interference. Wait, why didn't it taste like anything?" says Silt.

Lina just ignores him, irritating Silt more, though he calms down slightly and turns back over to Shadow. "Thanks Shadow, but why didn't you give me that earlier?" asks Silt.

"It was given to me by Yuki along with this crown," answers Shadow.

Silt is shocked while Lina can already tell he got it from Yuki after seeing the crown. "WHAT? And you made me drink it?! What if was poiso-HEY!" exclaims Silt, with Lina pulling him back to town.

With the other two walking back, Shadow decides to inspect the crown. It looks to be made of silver-colored metal with seven large gems adorning it. Taking a look at the inside of it, he notices a faded symbol on it. It's hard to make out. The closest Shadow can make out of it is an M with some bits of pink around it.

After finishing inspecting it, Shadow puts the crown into his cloak. Shadow then heads back to the city, catching up with the others. Shadow notices that Silt and Lina are done arguing about the elixir.

As the sun rises, Shadow, Lina, and Silt walk back into the city. They are walking to the inn that Shadow and Lina are staying at.

"Geez, it's already morning, that was harder than I thought," says Lina.

"What are you complaining about? All you did was stand on the sidelines during that whole fight," responds Silt, looking at Lina with an irritated look.

"Hey, I helped you two near the end," says Lina embarrassingly.

"Oh yeah, you threw a smoke bomb, you are the MVP of the battle," Silt responds, still irritated.

"Hey I know to not fight when the odds are against me," says Lina, starting to get irritated at Silt.

"Then why did you even bother passing through the force field after pushing Shadow and me!? Speaking of which, I'm still mad that you pushed us in the first place and for continually running away without answering my questions," says Silt.

"Firstly, I'm sorry about pushing you two in. I thought you were going in anyway so why did it matter? I went through because I needed to ask Yuki something as soon as I could. Secondly, I have no obligation to answer any of your, possibly stupid, questions," responds Lina.

"OH, is that why you ditched us while I was taking on my trial!?" asks Silt.

"I knew you would be fine, I saw you from Yuki's dining room, you stupid sandcastle!" responds Lina.

Silt and Lina continue to argue until they reach the inn.

"Well fine, let's get Shadow's opinion on the issue. Hey Shadow, what do you think, huh?" asks Lina, seeing Shadow is gone.

"Wait, wasn't he right behind us? When did he separate from us?" asks Silt.

Lina walks into the inn and heads to the front desk, thinking Shadow just went inside before them. Silt follows her, wondering what she's doing.

"Hello, did the man wearing mostly black with a covered face and a brown cloak come back in after he left last night?" asks Lina.

"Oh yes, he was here a few minutes ago. He already checked out and asked when the train would be leaving for Lust's territory. I told him that if he wanted to make it he should head there now. He thanked me and started heading to the station," explains the inn employee.

Lina and Silt look at each other, then back at the employee.

"Thanks, I'd like to check out right now," say Lina and Silt in unison.

After checking out, Lina and Silt walk out of the inn and start running to the train station.

At that moment Shadow is at the station buying his ticket for the train. *Ok, now to Lust. Hopefully it should be easier than Yuki, especially since he said he would let them know who I was. I really hope it just doesn't turn out to be a trap,* thinks Shadow.

While thinking this he notices that the devils around him are still giving him weird looks, but he just ignores it. While waiting to board he sees people being loaded onto the train. It's the sinners from Yuki's base. This is easy to tell since most of them have trees sprouting from them signifying their sins. They are all wrapped up in different colors covering their whole body, possibly to show which sin they are to be sent to next. Their eyes, mouth, and ears are all covered as best as they can be. A strange collar is around all of their necks with a strange writing on them and an even stranger aura coming from them. Trees of their sins are sprouting from their heads, chests, and backs. Their arms are bound with straightjackets and they have their legs either fully or partially bound, depending on if they can walk or not. Those that can't walk are being carried on flatbeds. Shadow also notices one without any trees on them, but they have a large white armband with a symbol of the sun on it. After what Lina told him yesterday Shadow can figure what is going to happen to that one. They are being loaded onto different-looking slightly bigger cars from the cars that are available. With all of this, what disturbs Shadow isn't the sinners, but the fact that no one is even paying much attention to them. They may as well be loading cargo onto the train with how the devils ignore them. For Shadow it all seems familiar.

I guess some things are the same whether on earth or in hell, thinks Shadow.

While thinking, he starts to hear a noise that is becoming louder. Shadow looks to where the noise is coming from and he sees Lina and Silt running toward the station. They see Shadow and go to him. When they reach him they both look at him, slightly irritated.

"Hey Shadow, why'd you ditch us?" ask Lina and Silt at the same time.

"You two were arguing and it was faster to walk by myself. Plus why does it matter? I was always planning to head to Lust's territory. It was only because of you, Lina, that we ended up in that situation to begin with," responds Shadow.

Lina starts giving a guilty look while Silt gets right next to Shadow.

Plus after that fight I know for certain who you really are Lina, thinks Shadow.

Silt, trying to break the awkwardness, walks up to Shadow. "Come on, don't be like that. We ended up doing great there. Plus, hearing what your goal is, I want to help you like you did for me, so we should team up and tackle this adventure together," says Silt, walking up right next to Shadow. Silt then slaps Shadow on his back as a sign of friendship.

Within a matter of seconds Shadow gets behind Silt and places his sword next to his neck.

Silt looks at Lina with both confusion and fear on his face.

"Oh yeah, it seems he doesn't like it when people touch his back," says Lina.

"You couldn't have told me that earlier Lina?! Look Shadow, I'm sorry, I didn't mean to make you uncomfortable," says Silt with fear in his voice.

While it's out, Lina looks at Shadow's sword, and remembers the aura that wrapped around it during the fight with Yuki and now notices its condition. The sword isn't the best quality, but it is still usable, though after the fight it shows some damage, mainly a few hairline cracks.

"Figures. That sword doesn't look like it will last long. He needs something stronger to handle whatever that power is. Maybe I should tell him to get a new one before it breaks. Though thinking about it, that power he used gives me a sense of déjà vu, but from where? thinks Lina.

While Lina is thinking about all of this, Shadow calms down, then puts his sword away and backs away from Silt. "It's fine, and I'm sorry, that was mostly a reflex. Also, if you two want to join me I'm not going to stop you. Though you should get your tickets because I'm leaving on that train with or without you," says Shadow as he points to the ticket counter.

Lina and Silt look over to the ticket counter and the two race each other to get their tickets. While they leave to get their tickets Shadow boards the train.

While this happens a message is sent out to all of the sins from Yuki. In his message he explains everything he knows about Shadow, including his current skills, his strange ability, who is traveling with him, and what he's after. The message is received by most of the sins, though the leading sin of Sloth has a problem about what she's heard. It isn't about the strange ability or his traveling companions, it's about how fast Shadow has progressed already. She in fact planned for most of this except his fast growth.

She motions behind her, where there are two human-sized containers and someone that works under her. The subordinate takes one of the two containers. The one they grab is labeled to go to Wrath. As it is taken away Sloth sighs heavily and starts to rework her plan with this new information, then realizes that her other subordinate happens to be in Lust's territory to compare data. She becomes both worried and hopeful that they'll be fine and possibly gather more data on Shadow when he gets there.

After getting their tickets they are somewhat annoyed since the only seats left are next to each other. After boarding the train Lina and Silt get to their seats. The train car they walk into has normal seats and some private rooms near the front of the car.

"Ugh, why did I have to sit next to you?" asks Silt.

"It can't be helped, the morning train is mostly used to move sinners, so there are few passenger cars, meaning there are few seats available to devils and stupid sandcastles like you," responds Lina, giving Silt a smug look.

"Why, you no good, useless—wait, where's Shadow again? Don't tell me he really ditched us again," says Silt.

"It shouldn't be that hard to find him, these are the only two train cars with seats for passengers on this run," says Lina. The two of them look around the cart and they don't see him.

After the train gets on its way the two of them get up from their seats to go look for him. They look through the car they are in and don't find him, then move to the other car. They pass by the private rooms in their car. One of them has its windows covered and the door locked, which the two pay no mind to. They just pass it and go to the next car, but unbeknownst to them, that's where Shadow is. He paid more to get that room so that he could be by himself.

Now that he is alone he can finally relax enough and try to get some rest before getting to Lust's territory.

One down, six to go, thinks Shadow as he starts to nod off while sitting up in his seat.

On top of the train is the birdlike demon right above where Shadow is sleeping. It wants to stay close to him and keep an eye on him.

Meanwhile, in a location far from Shadow, Lina, and Silt...

In an old abandoned castle something starts happening. In the middle of the great hall of the castle sits a seven-point star. Two unknown beings are also within the hall, one sitting on a throne and the other standing next to them. The one sitting is decrepit beyond recognition and appears dead. The other seems rather healthy and provides care for the being on the throne. Suddenly one of the points begins to shine, a purple light engulfing the hall. The mysterious being looks at the light, then looks at the being on the throne. Some light returns to their eyes. Though still decrepit they move slightly. They look at the star and start to chuckle.

"One down six to go," says the mysterious being.

About the Author

Devin Manbeck is the author of A Shadow's Journey: Prides Desire. A native of Kansas, he's loved stories across games, movies, and books all his life. His first book is a fulfillment of his dream to write a story that might one day entertain and engross others the way he was at such a young age. When he's not writing about the underworld, he's going on long walks and taking pictures of nature.